HEALING THE HURT

Tammy Morgan has lost her man, her best friend and very nearly her own life in a short space of time. Struggling to get back on track, and raising her son Toby alone, she makes sure Toby has everything he wants — except a daddy. Then Tammy's ex, Jason Rivera, returns home from Afghanistan, a changed man. Have the mental and physical scars of both their lives healed enough to enable them to rekindle the love they once had for each other?

CHARLOTTE McFALL

HEALING THE HURT

Complete and Unabridged

LINFORD
Leicester

First published in Great Britain

First Linford Edition
published 2014

A catalogue record for this book is available
from the British Library.

ISBN 978–1–4448–2044–7

Published by
F. A. Thorpe (Publishing)
Anstey, Leicestershire

Set by Words & Graphics Ltd.
Anstey, Leicestershire
Printed and bound in Great Britain by
T. J. International Ltd., Padstow, Cornwall

This book is printed on acid-free paper

2007

Tammy wasn't sure what she was doing, but it was the only way. Well, the only thing she could think of. She had asked Jason to meet her at the Bay Horse for a drink. Her parents would call it a need for Dutch courage. That was definitely something she was going to need. She could see that this was a big mistake, but Jason had to go. Tammy entered the pub and looked around. Jason hadn't arrived yet, so she paid for two lagers and took them over to a table near the door. A quick escape would be a must, or else any resolve she had would crumble.

Tammy had lost all sense of time and had stopped paying attention to her surroundings.

'Tam.'

Tammy looked up and saw Jason towering above her, dressed in his green gardening uniform.

'Sit down, Jason.' Her voice was uneven.

'What's up?' he replied. He looked confused. *Here goes,* she thought.

'Jason, go and join the army. It's what you want to do. Just . . . ' Tammy paused. Her voice was uneven but she needed to say it. 'You will be doing it without me.'

'Tam, don't be daft. Come on, I love you.'

Tammy stood up and walked around the table towards the exit. 'Well I don't love you.' The words caught in her throat. 'I never want to see you again.' She didn't give him a chance to retaliate; Tammy knew if she did, he would discover her lie.

She hurried out of the door jumped in her car and drove off, tears falling silently down her face. Tammy knew she would always love Jason. Although, why had she thought breaking up with him would be the only way for him to follow his dream? It was beyond even her comprehension, but no doubt she would get over it one day. Hopefully Jason wouldn't hate her forever; she had done it for him. Someone as handsome as he was would easily find another girlfriend.

It had been a long, torturous four months since she had seen Jason. Now here she was, sat at the back of the crowd, watching with pride as the new army recruits passed through. The drill sergeant shouted for them to present arms. It was as if they were all working as one as they thrust their weapons towards the crowd. The families clapped, and Tammy cheered and clapped with them. She had to admit that they all looked extremely handsome in their green number two dress uniforms and peak caps. Everywhere she looked she saw the insignia of the Duke of Lancaster Regiment adorning berets, peak caps and flags. The bright red rose of Lancashire, topped off with a crown, was displayed with pride wherever she looked.

Tammy's heart swelled with pride for Jason, and just for that one brief moment she felt it hadn't been a mistake. Unfortunately, Jason's dream had come at a huge cost to her. Tammy's own heart was totally broken, and she couldn't see how anything would change that. There wouldn't be anyone else; she would always love Jason. If he ever came home on leave, though, she would need to keep up the pretence and make sure he went back to where he was stationed. Even if it meant being horrible to him, she wasn't going to stand in his way.

1

Tammy stood in the queue, thoroughly enjoying the view in front.

'Tasty.' She kept her voice low, but apparently not low enough.

'I know,' was the cocky reply.

Tammy felt the heat rising on her face. She couldn't believe she had just said that aloud.

The deep voice struck a harmonious chord in her mind, but she struggled to place it. The flush travelled from her cheeks to her neck, whilst the voice in her head gave a stark warning. *Looking is OK, Tammy. Just don't ever get close to anyone; no one will want you now.*

The owner of the fatigue-covered butt turned to look her in the eye. 'Hi, Tammy.'

'Jason,' was the only reply she could give.

'Nice to see you; what are you doing here?'

Tammy knew she should reply, but her brain wasn't working the way it should. She had no idea why after all these years he had turned up again. Panic made her defensive, but her tone was even. 'If it's all right with you, I'm in a fast food restaurant waiting to be served. What does it look like?'

Jason raised his eyebrow, causing her stomach to whirl around like a washing machine on a spin cycle. How was she supposed to eat anything now? She watched as Jason's eyes roamed over her body. She desperately wanted to know what he was thinking, but he had shut himself off from her years ago.

'How have you been?' he asked.

'Fine!' Tammy wanted the conversation to end here. She didn't like it that he could still send shivers running up and down her spine. His enigmatic blue eyes made her lose all sense of reality. She had to go — be anywhere except around Jason Rivera. Dropping her eyes to the tiled floor, she spied his kit bag leaning against his leg.

'I see you're still a squaddy.'

He stood nearly motionless, his arms folded across his chest and feet slightly apart. 'Yes, I am, but I'm on leave.' Could he be any more defensive?

She wasn't an expert in body language, but he may as well have hung a 'closed' sign around his neck. Tammy knew they hadn't seen each other for a few years, but his abruptness shocked her. It was obvious he didn't want to talk about it. She caught the look of sadness in his eyes. It was as though he was running from ghosts. It distressed her. She wasn't sure if her already jangled nerves could take much more. Tammy prayed that the woman behind the counter would serve Jason quickly, and he would leave her alone.

She glanced nervously around the crowded restaurant. It was lunchtime, and the place was packed to the gunnels. There were a few spare tables, but if she had to share with him, she was going to take hers to go.

'Next, please!'

The shout from the assistant took Jason's attention, much to Tammy's relief. He was looking at her far too closely, like he was looking for something. Well, whatever it was, he wasn't going to find it here.

Jason placed his order, quickly turning back around; he didn't want Tammy to go anywhere, at least not yet. 'Look, as we're both getting food, why don't we sit together?' Jason's arm waved casually over to the few empty tables. 'It's always nice to catch up with old friends.'

'There is somewhere I need to be. I can't be late.' Tammy checked her watch. 'I have to leave in half an hour.'

'Where are you going?' If she was so intent on running away, he needed to know why.

She managed to reply through tight lips. 'Nowhere special; I just need to be somewhere. Let's just leave it at that.'

If he was going to shut down on her,

then she could certainly play the same game. She would keep her mouth shut. Besides, what business was it of his? Did he think he was going to come waltzing back into her life and assume they were going to pick up where they left off? *Think again, Army Boy. Blow that for a game of soldiers.*

As Tammy paid for her own order, the left sleeve of her cardigan rolled up. As she scrambled to pull it back down; she could feel the tears sting the backs of her eyes. *No one can see that; no one,* she chastised herself.

'It will just be good to catch up. I have been away so long. I have no idea what everyone is up to these days.' He gave a half smile, but she noticed it didn't reach his eyes. He looked like a hollowed-out version of the Jason she'd known before. Yes, army life had made a man out of him physically: his shoulders were broader, his arms more muscular, his butt . . .

'What do the stripes mean?' Tammy asked, pointing to his shoulder. 'Have you been anywhere exciting?' Anywhere had to be more exciting than the small town where she lived. And if she asked him questions, her mind wouldn't wander to what might have been.

'I'm a corporal.' Jason felt as if he was cornered, hunted. If he still knew Tammy at all, she wasn't going to let this drop. 'It isn't exciting at all.' He tried to swallow the lump that lingered in his throat. He was happy to be home and not in Helmand; he didn't want to go back, but he knew that he would have to someday. He'd lost enough friends over the past few months as it was. He dreaded the thought of holding a comrade in his arms, watching his life fade away. The mere thought of it tightened his stomach.

Jason was glad he had seen Tammy, but he wasn't sure that the feeling was mutual. She didn't seem pleased to see him, yet she had been admiring his behind. A wry smile crossed his lips; she still wore the wacky hippy clothes and had a penchant for purple. He'd always liked that about her; she was never afraid to be different. Tammy never wanted to be a part of the fashion crowd; she preferred to stand alone.

She was still nice to look at, yet there was something different about her. It was nothing obvious, nothing he could put his finger on and say, yeah, that's it. She held herself differently. Her shoulders were rounded; her hands fluttered around her arms close to her sides, as if she wanted to hold herself, and the sparkle that used to light her eyes had been extinguished.

The conversation was becoming strained; it wasn't like him not to have anything to say. 'Are you staying with your parents?' she asked him. Surely he would answer this question — or would he avoid it altogether? Tammy got the feeling Jason was getting good at avoiding things. She saw the forced smile he gave her.

'Yes, I'm staying with my parents. Nothing beats Mum's cooking.'

Tammy nodded her head in agreement. 'Your mum could always make a mean Sunday roast.' Her stomach twisted in knots; she had always been in tune with Jason when they were younger. Now, he seemed hollow; something was wrong.

If he didn't want to talk about it, then she knew better than to press him for information. She had forgiven him long ago for what happened between them — not that he had a choice. When she looked up at him, her heart pounded against her ribcage, threatening to escape. She definitely didn't need any more complications in her life, especially from men. Every day was an uphill struggle for her to function normally, if that was what she could call it.

A quick meal with Jason, then they would both go their separate ways. Grabbing her food, she walked over to the seating area. Tony's wasn't the most upmarket takeaway, with its plastic chairs and old melamine tables, but their Hawaiian burgers were her idea of nirvana. Jason swung his kitbag over his shoulder and grabbed his tray of food. He waited until she had taken her seat before he seated himself.

'I thought Debbie might have been with you.'

Tammy caught the way Jason looked around the restaurant. She knew what he was thinking — that Debbie would just jump out at him. How Tammy wished that could be true.

'You two were always together,' he continued.

Tammy saw that Jason walked with a slight limp. What was up with that? She wondered.

'Debbie's not here anymore.' Tammy looked down and studied the cracks in the table. It was the truth.

'Where has she gone?'

'Let's drop it. I don't want to talk about it anymore.' Her voice was barely a whisper.

'Would your aunt and uncle know her address?' He didn't seem to want to let it go. She hoped even more that the clock would tick by, and she would be able to leave. Well, at least she had a valid excuse.

'Just drop it Jason please! Don't go and see them. They don't need to be bothered.' Her aunt and uncle hated her anyway, and she didn't go around anymore. They had never said anything like that to her, but she knew they did.

Jason looked at Tammy. He couldn't believe what he was hearing; after all, Debbie and Tammy were cousins as well as best friends. What had happened to tear them apart? He couldn't blame her for not confiding in him. He wanted to find a much safer subject — anything other than what had happened in the army. He couldn't talk about that, not to anyone; the M.O.D. had sent him off home to recover. Could anyone recover from that? He wasn't sure, but he would give it a damn good shot. He had plans and none of them included having a woman around to drag him down and get in his way. Looking at

14

Tammy made him wish he hadn't made that decision; she still made the hairs on the back of his neck stand on end.

'What's wrong with your leg?' Tammy asked whilst trying to decide if she should eat a french fry, or leave her dinner entirely.

'Nothing; I twisted it, that's all. It hasn't healed properly yet.'

Tammy checked her watch for the umpteenth time. She couldn't be late and leave him standing all alone whilst his friends had gone home. 'Jason, I've really got to go.'

'You've hardly touched your dinner.'

'I wasn't as hungry as I thought I was.' *Can't he get the message I'm not interested in making polite small talk with someone I don't know anymore?*

'I thought we could put the past behind us.'

Tammy sighed loudly. 'Jason, it doesn't matter what happened back then; I hope it's all forgiven and forgotten, as they say.'

Dinner was the last thing on

Tammy's mind. Jason was asking too many questions — questions that she hoped she'd never have to answer. She hated the fact that he had chosen the army over her, but at least she could understand now why he made the decision he had. They needed people like him — reliable, strong, people who would put their fellow soldiers first before themselves.

Pity he couldn't put me first, she thought. A black forbidding shadow had hung over her for years. Tammy pushed herself to a standing position making her point to leave.

'If you really have to go, why not let me walk with you?' he asked, his face expressionless.

Tammy kept her voice even. 'Ok, but you can only walk with me so far, and then you have to leave,' she replied in the sternest voice she could 'Is it a deal?' Her heart was still racing and she could feel her flesh colour.

'Sure thing, my lady.'

A cool breeze hit them as they

walked out into the fresh air. The shopping precinct was busier than usual; Tammy put it down to the gleaming red fire engine parked on the pavement. Children, helped by two burly firemen, scrambled to climb onto it.

'Tammy!'

Tammy turned instinctively to see who had shouted at her. One of the firemen waved frantically, trying to garner her attention. She walked over to him as quickly as she could.

'Hi Stan.' Tammy leaned over and kissed him briefly on the cheek.

A pang of jealousy hit Jason as he saw the first genuine smile grace Tammy's face — and it was for this fireman, not for him. The man hugged her. *That's a bit much; who does he think he is?* Tammy was his girl, not some fireman's who looked old enough to be her father. Jason checked himself. *No, she isn't your girl anymore, and she hasn't been for a long time.* He had to keep reminding himself who broke up with whom. Ever since he had joined the army, he had locked his emotions away in a dark, dank cupboard. Seeing Tammy today had stirred things in him that he hadn't been sure he could feel anymore.

'Are you two still on for tomorrow?' Stan asked whilst trying to prise a child from his leg.

'Of course, Stan; we're really looking forward to it.'

Tammy watched as Stan gave Jason the once-over. 'Is your friend coming?'

'No, Stan, he's not,' Tammy replied through tight lips.

'The more the merrier, I say. It's better if a lot of people turn up, Tammy. You know that.'

Jason held out his hand to the man. 'Hi, I'm Jason. Looks like you're having fun there,' he said, pointing to the children climbing all over the engine.

'Stan Uttley. It's a pleasure. You boys deserve a medal for what you're doing over there.'

'To be honest, I don't really do anything special.' Jason tried to deflect the attention away from himself and back onto the fireman. 'So, what's happening tomorrow?'

'It's the annual fire service fundraiser. Tammy here helps me out, serving refreshments and such. Here, take a leaflet.'

'Jason's just come back from tour; he will have other more important things to do than come to our fundraiser,' Tammy snapped back.

Jason quickly scanned the leaflet. It seemed like a good cause, and Tammy was going to be there. Stan had piqued his interest. Jason did wonder why Tammy hadn't wanted him to go and who she was so afraid he would see. If it wasn't Stan, then who the hell was she going to the fundraiser with? Maybe he'd come just to see if this man was right for his Tammy. He wouldn't have to follow her now; he could just bump into her here tomorrow. She seemed set against him attending. Well, wouldn't she be surprised? He shook his head. No doubt his parents and brother would be vying for his attention; he wasn't even sure if he'd told them he was coming home today.

'Stan, Jason, I best go. I'm definitely going to be late. I'll see you tomorrow at the station.'

Jason watched Tammy rush away from him. She was different; something had changed in her life. What was it with those silly cardigans? It wasn't even that cold! He remembered a vivacious woman always ready to try something new. But now, she seemed to have gone in the opposite direction — too quiet, too timid.

'Maybe I'll see you tomorrow,' said Jason.

'Well, you know where we are if you want to come,' replied Stan.

Jason threw his khaki kit bag over his shoulder and marched towards the taxi rank. He couldn't shake the feeling that he wasn't the only one who had changed, and this change wasn't one for the better either.

Four years in Afghanistan had scarred him; he'd come home rarely over the years, preferring to go back to the Weeton Barracks instead. When his family insisted he go home, he'd stayed in the house. He hadn't wanted to see anyone; it would have hurt too much. But after this last tour, things were different. This time he needed to be with friends and his family, to have fun and relax with people that he cared about, and who cared about him.

Tammy had meant everything to him, and she'd let him go, knowing how desperately he wanted to join the army. She'd never put up a fight to force him to choose between her and what he'd seen as his duty to queen and country. In fact, she had made the decision for him and he hadn't put up a fight to make her stay.

Jason hadn't bothered to write to her, preferring instead to make a clean break. Who was he kidding? It had been for his own selfish reasons that he hadn't kept in touch. He couldn't bear the thought of her with another man, and how happy they might be together, when he wanted her with him. But he had let her go. He had been hurt enough, and that was how it had to stay. Even if he had forgiven her, it wasn't fair to her. Once he was back on the front line, he didn't want Tammy waiting for a phone call, or people turning up on her doorstep telling her something had happened to him and he wouldn't be coming back.

Jason was curious about Tammy's date for the fundraiser, and he was determined to mention the event to his family. Perhaps they should all go; that way, it wouldn't look suspicious. Tammy couldn't have any objection if his whole family attending, could she?

★ ★ ★

Hitting the lunchtime traffic did little to improve Tammy's mood. Only the sight

22

of her favourite boy would do that; only he could ever manage to make her feel loved and wanted again. Toby didn't care what she looked like in the morning, or if she was having a bad day; he didn't even care about the way she looked without her cardigans.

As Tammy rounded the corner, the sign for Fresh Spring Nursery came into view. A group of parents were hanging around in the playground. Breathing a sigh of relief, Tammy was glad she wasn't late. She never wanted Toby to think she wasn't coming or that he would be left standing in the classroom alone.

She had a feeling she was being watched, but turning quickly, the only thing she could see was other parents arriving to collect their own children. She pulled into the car park and waited until the door opened. At last the kids came streaming out. As usual, Toby was one of the last ones through the door. His blond hair glinted in the sunlight as he ran towards her.

'Mummy, I made this for you.' He handed over his prized painting before flinging his arms around his mum.

'It's a beautiful picture, Toby. You're quite the artist. We'll put it on the fridge when we get home,' Tammy replied, hugging her son.

It always saddened Tammy when she saw Toby's pictures. They always included a mum, a dad, and a house. They had a house, but their family consisted of two; he'd never have a dad to play football with him. It wasn't his fault, but she couldn't help feeling guilty that what he wanted most was the one thing she'd never be able to give him. Tammy shook her head. She had to be truthful — that was the one thing she had taken away from Toby before he had had the chance of knowing it.

As they walked to the car hand in hand, a wave of contentment washed over her. Toby loved her no matter what, and that made her ecstatically happy. She secured him into his child seat. 'Are you looking forward to seeing the big red fire engines tomorrow?'

'Yes, Mummy! Fireman Stan said I could sit in the driving seat and drive.'

Tammy looked in the rear view mirror and smiled. 'That will be great, Toby, but I thought you were helping me give out the cakes?'

'No, Mummy; I want to play with the fire engine.'

Tammy saw Toby's lopsided grin and had to laugh herself. Well, he did have his priorities right — hand out cakes or have fun playing with a full-sized fire engine instead of a toy one. She owed a great deal to Spring's fire service, and this was her small way of repaying their kindness to her and to Toby. If all she did was help out on their fundraisers, she was doing her bit. All the men at the station seemed to have taken a shine to her son and were always happy to have him hanging around.

Everything should go like clockwork tomorrow as long as Jason didn't put in an appearance. A shiver ran down her spine. Why had seeing him again stoked the flames of passion in her? One touch from him had always turned her into a quivering wreck. Her inner voice shouted louder this time. *No, Tammy!* Tammy shook her head. This wouldn't do; she had to stop wishing things were different. The only thing she was capable of doing was making sure Toby had everything he could ever need — everything except the daddy that he so desperately wanted.

2

Tammy woke up the next morning feeling less than refreshed. She'd spent half the night going over the meeting with Jason. Even though she hadn't seen him in almost five years, he'd inadvertently brought back all those feelings she'd tried so hard to repress. Perhaps if she'd voiced her opinions more forcefully back then, he wouldn't have enlisted. She shook her head. No that wouldn't have worked. He'd been too determined to go and help, to do his duty as he'd seen it, and she'd stood in his way. So, Tammy had done the only thing she could and had moved aside. When he left, Jason had made it clear that there would be no contact. Well, at least that was what Debbie had said, and after she had dumped Jason like that she really couldn't blame him.

She looked through her wardrobe

and decided to forgo her signature colour and opted for a black gypsy skirt and top, together with a white cardigan. She smiled to herself. How would all the old dears take to being served by a woman garbed head to foot in deep purple? She was happy that Toby had gotten ready so easily this morning. He was excited about seeing the fire engines. They often made unexpected visits to the station to watch the men in action, or just sit in the front seat and turn the sirens on and off. Everything should be perfect today; but if Jason put in appearance, Tammy wasn't sure how she would explain it to Toby.

Looking out of the kitchen window, she saw dark, menacing clouds dancing in the sky. Tammy prayed quietly to herself that the rain wouldn't fall and dampen the day for all of them. The firemen needed to raise money, and if it rained, all of the outside events would have to be cancelled. The fun run would go ahead, and the refreshments were easily moved inside, but the children wouldn't be able to play in the bouncy castle or on the slide that was supposed to be there.

The roads were fairly quiet for a Saturday morning, and Tammy arrived in no time. Even though River Springs was a small town, there was always a good turn-out to support the boys who risked their lives each time they responded to a fire. She knew that, even with all her volunteering and cake-baking, she could never repay them for what they had done for Toby and her.

Stan was outside putting up the last of the bunting. The refreshment marquee had been erected, and three gleaming fire engines on the gravel waited for the children who would no doubt dull their shiny coats with mucky shoes and sticky hands.

As she stepped out of the car, she called over, 'Hey Stan, do you need a hand?'

'Aye,' he answered, his voice tinged with frustration. 'Every time I put this side of the bunting up, the other side falls down. It's a never-ending circle,' he replied, balancing on a small ladder.

'Wait here, Toby.' Walking over to the other side of the yard, Tammy grabbed the bunting off the ground and climbed a few steps up the ladder. 'Ready, Stan?' She waited until he had the bunting in the right place. 'Now!' she ordered and waited a few extra seconds on the ladder to make sure the bunting didn't fall down again.

Tammy pulled her sleeves down — not that she really needed to hide anything from Stan. He'd already seen how horrible her arms were and didn't care. All he cared about was that she and Toby were happy.

'Thanks, Tammy, love; I couldn't have done it without your help,' Stan said merrily as he climbed down the ladder.

As she looked around, Tammy saw that the yard was empty. 'Where is everyone?' She watched as Stan licked his lips.

'They're in the mess room, tucking

into Mrs Anderson's cakes.'

Tammy couldn't do anything but laugh. 'Those were for the refreshment stall; there'd better be some left.' She picked Toby up and carried him into the station, Stan following behind her.

Looking around the fire station, she could see that the dust fairies had been in and had spruced up the place. She headed straight into the mess room, intent on giving them what-for if they'd eaten everything. Opening the door quickly, she saw them all sitting around the large oak table, plates piled high with cakes and sandwiches. She coughed as loudly as she could, and stopped them in mid-bite.

'Come on boys; those are for the fundraiser, not for you lot to eat. Doesn't Mrs Anderson bring you enough treats as it is?' Tammy had to stifle a giggle when they all tried talking with their mouths full of cake.

'Mummy, why are they eating all the cakes?'

'Because they're greedy, Toby; they

couldn't wait until later.' Tammy did her best to sound stern, but failed miserably; everyone laughed at her feeble attempt. 'Come on, little man. Everyone will be arriving soon; you can come with me.' Stan held his arms out to the little boy. 'Be careful with him, Stan.'

'Tammy, how many years has Toby been coming here?' Stan said gruffly.

'All his life,' she conceded.

'Has anything happened to him whilst he has been here with us?'

'Well . . . ' Stan didn't give her a chance to finish.

'Exactly. Stop worrying for once and enjoy the party. The charity auction is going to be held tonight after the meal. Is your gran coming?'

Tammy realised how silly she was being. Toby would be safe; he was with a whole host of firemen quite capable of looking after a four-year-old.

'I'm sorry, Stan; you're right,' she replied, sighing. 'My gran is babysitting tonight; she said that a full day would be too much for her.'

The door from the kitchen swung open and Mrs Anderson appeared, loaded down with more cakes and sandwiches. 'Here you go boys; get some more down you,' she said as she placed another tray full of food on the table. She looked down at the floor and then turned her beady eye on one of the firemen. 'For goodness sake Roger, pick up your dirty T-shirt. You're not at home now, you know.'

Tammy tapped her foot in mock annoyance. 'Mrs Anderson, you'll spoil them.'

The firemen all looked at Tammy and laughed heartily.

'And I don't spoil both you and Toby when you come?' Mrs Anderson replied. This brought about more laughter from her friends.

'That's true; we never eat tea when we've been here, even for an hour.' Tammy loved Mrs Anderson. She was a contradiction, with her salt-and-pepper curls constantly covered by a hair net, and jeans and fancy-coloured tops. Tammy knew Mrs Anderson was right; anyone who came into the mess room, no matter who they were, would never leave hungry. She was like another grandma to them. The acceptance she found here at the station was something Tammy cherished; she'd believed she'd never find anyone else outside her family circle who could accept her as she was. They had all helped her through one of the most difficult periods of her life.

Tammy wandered back outside, where people had started arriving in droves. They stood behind the red tape, waiting patiently to peruse the stalls and enjoy the refreshments. Many of the children squealed with delight at the sight of the fire engines. She prayed that they would do well with their fundraising efforts today.

After Stan cut the ribbon and opened the event, Toby went off with Stan to play in the engines, and Tammy took her place in the refreshment tent. They were kept pretty busy with everyone clamouring to taste Mrs Anderson's fruit scones and cherry cake. The ladies didn't even have two minutes to sit down and rest their weary feet. Tammy was amazed that Mrs Anderson could keep going as she did.

Toby had been absent for most of the day, except when he wandered back over with one of the other lads in need of something to eat. He was far too busy to bother with her. For once, it was nice to have time to herself, and to be able to give something back. Not many people bothered volunteering.

Tammy was glad when the rush seemed to let up, and only a few people drifted in and out of the tent. She loved to look at the stalls and wanted to pick up a new book or a toy for Toby. By doing so, she was doing her part.

'Mrs Anderson, would you mind if I go and have a look around the stalls? We've gone pretty quiet.'

'Of course, dear; you run along. I will serve Mr Thompson and afterwards, I think I'll sit and have a nice cuppa myself.'

Tammy removed her apron and left it on a chair behind the counter. She thanked her and wandered off to look round.

★　★　★

Jason looked about him. He couldn't see Tammy, but there were so many people, it was difficult to find one person in particular. Now, what had Stan said she did? He racked his brain for the answer. Refreshments, of course! All he would have to do was look for the refreshment stand. Jason walked around the myriad stalls until he saw the marquee. People wandered out with plastic cups in one hand and slices of homemade cake in the other. He knew instantly that this was the right place. *Mmm, that fruit cake looks good,* he thought to himself, as his stomach growled.

Jason wondered if Tammy's attitude

towards him would've changed after yesterday's disastrous date. Why did he keep thinking of it as a date? She'd been in the fast food place just as he had; all he'd done was ask her to sit with him. Wandering over to the counter, he ordered a tea. 'It looks like you have a good turn-out,' said Jason, smiling.

The lady grabbed a cup and started pouring. 'Yes, we've been really busy here in the refreshment tent.'

Jason gave her his most flirtatious smile. 'It's all in the name of a good cause, isn't it?'

'Yes. Would you like milk?'

'Please. My friend said she was helping out here; I thought maybe she was doing refreshments.' He thought he was being rather sneaky, but it was a means to an end.

'What's your friend's name?'

'Tammy, Tammy Morgan.' Jason saw the woman eye him suspiciously. Would she tell him where Tammy was? More importantly, would she give him the name of her escort? He'd thought of nothing else since yesterday. He hadn't been to bed; he didn't sleep anymore. He couldn't face the dreams he had when he closed his eyes.

'How do you know our Tammy?' she asked guardedly. She certainly seemed protective; the smile on her face had disappeared.

'We used to date before I joined the army.' That was true, but the word 'date' seemed inadequate. They'd been friends, soul mates, and so much more.

'Oh, my dear, you're a soldier. Here have a scone.'

He coughed to hide his grin. What was it with people? One moment they were suspicious of your motives, and the next, when you told them that you served your country, they looked at you differently, as if they could trust you with anything. They wouldn't, if they realised how horrible it was over there — the heat, sand that got everywhere, and worse still, the fact that you didn't know who the enemy was. The lady in the market square could have been an insurgent for all anyone knew.

'Tammy said she was bringing a date,' he mumbled. 'I thought I'd give him the once-over to make sure he's right for her, you understand?' Jason couldn't believe how overprotective he sounded, especially for someone he hadn't seen for years.

'Oh, he's over by the fire engine; has been all day,' replied Mrs Anderson.

Jason paid for his tea, took his scone, and left the marquee. He could hear the woman's laughter following him across the yard. He wandered over to the engines, where he saw the fireman he'd met yesterday. 'Hi Stan,' he said.

'Jason, glad you could make it.'

'The lady in the refreshment tent told me I could find Tammy's date here.' He didn't want to mince his words. 'I want to make sure he's right for her.' Jason didn't understand the smirk Stan gave him.

'Ah, yes, Tammy's date; he's in the driver's seat. Between you and me, I'm positive he's perfect for her.' Stan grinned.

'Thanks.' Jason reluctantly wandered over to the engine cab, his heart pounding in his chest. He wanted to see who had captured her heart, but when he looked in the cab, all he saw was a little boy pretending to drive. Jason climbed off the step and walked quickly back over to Stan.

'It's a kid.' Jason was gobsmacked.

Stan laughed heartily. 'Of course it's a kid, who did you expect? Tammy doesn't date.'

Jason was astounded. A child? Her date was a little boy? He couldn't be over five. 'I thought she was dating a fireman.'

Stan shrugged his shoulders. 'No, lad. If you've any interest in her, you'll find it hard to get past the barriers she's erected.'

'We used to date a few years ago. Tammy seems a lot different now.'

'Aye, lad, people have told me. I've only known her the way she is now. I wish I'd known her back then.'

Jason would have stood there all day telling him about the old Tammy, but the girl they'd been discussing appeared out of nowhere. 'Tammy,' he said and smiled. He saw her fold her arms protectively.

'What are you doing here?'

He shrugged his shoulders. 'I thought I'd stop by.' It was the truth, wasn't it? Guilt forced him to speak honestly. 'Ok, you want the truth? I was curious. I wanted to know who'd come with you, and all I discovered was a little boy.'

'It's none of your concern.' She called to the child. 'Toby, come on, love. We'll go get some food.' Tammy held out her hand.

'Actually, Tammy, I think you and your friend need to talk. I'll take Toby to get something.' Stan lifted Toby down from the engine, and together they wandered off, leaving Tammy and Jason alone.

Jason just stared at her. He couldn't

believe Tammy hadn't mentioned any-thing about this yesterday. 'Well, it certainly didn't take long for you to move on, did it?' He saw Tammy flinch as his words struck their mark with lethal accuracy.

'It's not want you think! Toby isn't mine; he's Debbie's son.' The words flew out of her mouth before she could stop them.

Folding his arms across his chest, he sighed heavily. 'Why is he with you, if he is Debbie's son?'

'Debbie isn't here to look after him anymore; he's been with me ever since he was born.' A tear trickled down her face. 'Toby thinks that I'm his mum, so everyone just leaves it at that.' Tammy couldn't believe what she was saying. She had to keep up the pretence, even now, years later.

Jason didn't know what to think. Tammy still wasn't being forthcoming with information. He would just have to let it go for now. Something didn't seem right; what was she hiding? There had to be more to it than this, especially as she was fiddling with her hands like she used to when she was trying to hide something.

'So, what did Debbie do, just up and leave then?'

Tammy's tears flowed faster now. 'Please Jason, just stop asking questions.' Tammy turned her face away from him. 'It doesn't matter. Just go; I've had enough.'

He walked slowly towards her. He didn't really know what to do; Tammy was upset, and he didn't know why, except that it had to do with Debbie. Maybe Debbie felt she couldn't be a mum to her little boy. He pulled Tammy against his shoulder and let her weep, offering what little comfort he could. When her sobs finally abated, she abruptly moved away from him as if she had been burnt.

'I'm sorry. I've no idea why I did that.' *Yes, you do, Tammy; you know exactly why you have just done that.* Great! That stupid voice was back again. When would the voice leave her alone? Next time, she'd start calling it Jiminy Cricket!

'Tammy, why can't you tell me what's wrong?' Tammy bent her head low and Jason placed a finger under her chin, lifting her head up.

'I don't want to talk about it.' Her eyes were wide with fear. 'Can we just leave it, please? I'm begging you to let it drop, Jason.' Why on earth did she think this was the right thing to do? 'I don't see why you are so concerned about it; you can't come waltzing back here after all these years and start prying into my life.'

Jason could only let it go for now. But he'd find out, by any means necessary, what had happened to her. What had made her so sad and withdrawn? Her chocolate-brown eyes were dull and lifeless. In the brief time he'd been with her, he noticed that Toby was the only one who could make them shine.

'Listen, about this auction thing

tonight.' Jason paused. 'How about a bet?'

'What sort of bet?' she asked slowly. She felt her resolve crumbling.

'If I win the fun run, you have to come to the meal and auction with me.' He thought he saw a look of horror flash across her face. 'Just as friends, I promise. Deal?' he added quickly. Jason didn't feel guilty about using underhand tactics; he was convinced that he would win the fun run. How many of them were as fit as a soldier? Even with a limp, he had always had the fastest time going round the assault course.

'If you win the fun run, then yes,' Tammy reluctantly agreed.

Suddenly a loud crash resonated around the car park. Jason jumped, the hairs on his arms pricked up, and he immediately threw himself to the ground, his face inches away from the concrete.

'Jason, what are you doing?' Tammy held out her hand to help him to his feet. 'Someone's dropped a metal tray, that's all.'

What the hell was wrong with him? Why on earth did he think lying flat on the floor would do any good? Someone had dropped something; there were no bombs or grenades, no gunfire. *Pull yourself together Jason, or you're going to make a bigger fool of yourself than you already have.* He flinched at every noise he heard. No matter how hard he'd tried, he couldn't erase the memories. Were the insurgents back? Were they hiding, waiting just around the corner, ready to pounce? They hadn't completed the job when he'd left Afghanistan; maybe they'd come to England to finish it. Jason shook his head, trying desperately to suppress the thoughts.

Tammy couldn't believe that he had dropped to the floor like that because someone dropped a tray. She heard a mumbled 'I'm sorry' come from his direction.

'Don't worry about it. Just get up;

everyone is staring at us.' Tammy's hand was still outstretched.

Jason grabbed it and jumped quickly to his feet, but let her hand drop quickly and brushed down the front of his jeans. 'So, do we have a bet? When does this fun run start?'

'It starts in a few minutes; the start line is over there.' Tammy pointed in the direction as people were already lining up to start. 'If you win — and it's a big if — then I agree to go with you, but just as friends, nothing else.'

Jason didn't mistake the warning in her voice. 'That's cool.' He was one step closer to having his friend back. Sadly, that's all they could be, but his stomach wouldn't settle down around her. Every time he was near her, electricity seemed to arc in the air between them. Was he the only one who felt it, or did Tammy feel it too? Before he could find the answer to that question, he'd have to win this fun run. He looked around at the other runners. They varied from the very young, pushed in prams, to senior citizens. Judging by the competition, he felt positive that he'd win. 'See you at the finish line, Tammy!' Jason shouted confidently as the race starter shouted, 'Ready, set, go!'

The race started with everyone huddled together, trying to find their own rhythm. It wasn't a taxing circuit, simply twice around the station grounds. Jason paced himself as he continued to pass the other runners. He didn't care if people noticed he didn't quite run the way he should. He chuckled inwardly as he passed a fireman dressed up as a panda. The more people he passed along the way Jason knew, the better his odds were of winning his cheeky bet with Tammy. She'd been a sucker for bets and generally lost, and he always made sure she paid a forfeit. Occasionally, if he'd been feeling extremely generous, he'd let her win just to stop her from being too grumpy with him.

He checked his watch. Ten minutes — he'd been slow. Running wasn't something he did a lot of anymore, but he had to admit it was a lot easier running without fifty-five pounds strapped to his back. Making the final turn around the firehouse, he saw the finish line. He sped up and passed the only person in front of him. Tammy stood to one side, watching him, as the rest of the audience clapped and cheered the racers home. As they crossed the finish line, medals were handed out to all the participants.

He jogged over to her. 'I'll come and pick you up, if you would like. Do you still live at your mum's?'

She shook her head. 'No, Toby and I have our own place.' After giving him her address, Tammy went to find Toby. She looked briefly over her shoulder and saw Jason still standing where she'd left him. *Tammy, what are you doing?* That annoying voice was back. *I'm only going to the auction and buffet with him, it's not like I'm planning to run away.*

A bet was a bet, and she always fell for them like the idiot she was. One of these days, she'd make him pay for every stupid bet she'd had lost. Maybe she should cancel and make him go on his own. That wouldn't be fair; besides, she'd left a huge wet patch on the shoulder of his T-shirt. It wasn't like they were going to be on their own anyway. Tammy would have to keep telling herself it wasn't a date.

As she wandered back to the refreshment tent in search of Toby, Tammy tried to convince herself that everything was going to be okay. No matter how she looked at it, there was no way she could get out of going to the charity auction with Jason. She owed too much to the fire station to let them down; also, she was the one taking all the bids. People had offered their services to the highest bidders to help the retirement home for ex and injured servicemen.

Mrs Anderson sat with Toby as she

plied him with food. 'That looks like a good dish, Mrs A.'

'Speaking of nice dishes, there was a nice young man looking for you. He seemed desperate to know who your date was.'

Tammy wished that Mrs Anderson would stop trying to match-make. She'd set her up with one of the lads on the watch, but they were all like brothers to her. 'He's an old friend, just returned from tour. I wouldn't agree with you about him being a dish though.' Tammy hoped her lie was believable.

Jason had always been attractive. How many times had she enjoyed his strong arms wrapped around her? She couldn't help but wonder what it would be like to be held like that by someone who loved her. It was all very well that Toby gave her hugs, but it wasn't the same as being embraced by Jason. Where had that come from, she wondered? That won't be happening again, Tammy told herself.

You put paid to that.

'Come on, Tammy; tell me how you really know him,' Mrs Anderson probed.

'We used to go out, but we split up when he joined the army.' Tammy smiled indulgently. 'See? There's nothing to tell.'

'He still seems to be sweet on you; you can see it in his eyes.' Tammy noticed the faraway look on Mrs Anderson's face. 'I liked a soldier once upon a time.' She seemed lost in the memory.

Tammy covered her mouth with her hand trying to hide the smile appearing on her face.

'He was a G.I.; such a handsome young man. He took me to a few dances and to the flicks. Sadly, he died during the war. I met Mr Anderson a while later, and as they say, the rest is history.'

Tammy had never known Mrs Anderson's age, but realised that she must have been no more than sixteen during the war. She still kept going and ran around after the fireman as if she were their mother. If she had half the energy that this lady did when she was her age, Tammy would be happy.

'Jason asked me to go to the auction with him, so I told him he could give me a lift.'

'Come on, tell me more. Why didn't things work out with you two?' Mrs Anderson's interest was definitely aroused. There wasn't much going on, and all the boys and Tammy were her extended family. She always liked to know what was going on; it gave her something to gossip about with the other women down at the WRVS.

'He wanted to enlist in the army, and there was no room for me in his life, so I let him go,' Tammy replied sadly.

Mrs Anderson winked at her. 'I think you made a mistake letting him go.'

Tammy didn't like the way the conversation was going. She needed to change the subject, and quickly. 'Come on, we'd best clear all these tables.' She picked up a dish cloth to emphasize her point and wandered from table to table, cleaning off all the crumbs and collecting the dirty dishes. She'd take them into the fire station and wash them. She pointed to the pile of dirty plates and cups she'd collected. 'Mrs Anderson, I'll just go and take care of these.'

Tammy wanted this conversation to end without further enlightening Mrs Anderson. Honestly, the woman was like a dog with a bone. She could never let anything interesting drop.

'Don't be silly dear. Don't you need to go off and make yourself pretty for that nice young man?'

'I have plenty of time for that, so I will do all the dishes.' She nodded towards the others. 'I know the lads are good at eating your food, but they are utterly useless at cleaning up after themselves.' She chuckled and walked away with her full tray.

It had been a good day. People had started wandering away, but they'd show up at the community centre later. All the calendars had sold out; it had taken less than ten minutes for them all to go. Who wouldn't want pictures of hunky firemen on their wall? Okay, maybe they weren't all drop-dead gorgeous, but, as they say, there was someone for everyone. Only once all the money was counted would they know if they'd made enough to finally break ground on the new building.

Tammy put the dirty dishes in the sink, staring at all the bubbles popping and swirling around in the water. Jason was back and she had to protect Toby at all costs; she wouldn't allow Jason to hurt her son.

No, she should know him well enough to know he wouldn't do that, but she wouldn't allow her secrets to get out. Why had she just agreed to go out on a date with him? She could try and make out that it wasn't a date, but the facts were he was going to be picking her up at her own house and escorting her to the auction. Tammy looked at her watch; it wasn't going to be long before she was back in his company. Her pulse still hadn't stopped racing, and the butterflies in her stomach wouldn't settle down. Jason Rivera had a lot to answer for; she hadn't been able to think straight since she had seen him again. Even the washing up was going slowly, as he invaded her every thought.

3

The fundraiser had been a huge success, but there was still plenty of money to be raised. The meal wouldn't be gourmet fare by any means, just homemade meat and potato pie and mushy peas, but it always went down well. The lads enjoyed their home cooked food; who didn't?

After dropping Toby off at her grandmother's house, Tammy drove back to her own to get ready. What she really wanted was to phone Jason and call the whole thing off. The voices in her head were getting louder, the warnings more forceful. A sense of dread filled her. Shaking her head, she forced her way through the traffic. Why did he still have to look so good? Even the army-style haircut hadn't done anything to diminish his good looks.

She and Toby were okay as a happy

family of two, as happy as they could be. Tammy knew that Toby wanted a father. When Father's Day had come round, he'd produced a wonderful card for his granddad, but she knew that it wasn't the same since unlike his friends, he couldn't send it to his own father.

When she pulled into the driveway, she looked up and down the street to see if Jason was there already, waiting for her. She wasn't sure if he was coming on foot or borrowing his parents' car. She was almost positive that he didn't have a car of his own. What would be the point of letting it sit on the driveway until he came home on leave?

For the next hour, Tammy searched through her wardrobe trying to choose the perfect outfit to wear. She had thrown all the unsuitable garments on her bed, and soon there were more clothes covering her duvet than still hung on the rails. She laughed; since when did it take this long to pick out an outfit? Nothing she chose seemed right for this date.

She shook her head. *It isn't a date. We're both going to the same place. Jason is just giving me a lift.* At least that was what Tammy tried to tell herself. It wasn't going to be a posh auction. Yes, the mayor would be there, and a reporter from the local paper, but that was it.

Finally Tammy picked out an outfit, again deciding to forgo her all purple ensemble in favour of a classic black Spanish skirt and matching gypsy top. She finished off her outfit with a long-sleeved purple jacket. Looking in the mirror, she felt as if someone else were staring back at her. Hardly anyone saw her without a cardigan or wearing makeup; she didn't see the point of all that messing about.

A knock on the door interrupted her thoughts. Grabbing her handbag, she flew downstairs; she didn't want Jason to come inside. Tammy realised what he was awakening inside her, but she couldn't allow herself to be swept away on a tidal wave of emotion.

'Hi, Tammy.' Jason stood on the doorstep dressed in slacks and a crisp white shirt. She couldn't help herself tracing the contours of his muscles with her eyes.

She didn't miss Jason's own obvious examination and approval of her. 'Hi. You sure you want to come?'

'I told your friend I would. Besides, who else is going to chauffer you?'

Tammy kept her voice steady and even. 'I'm quite capable of driving myself.'

Jason held up his hand; maybe he was being a little bit too pushy. *Keep it cool, Jason,* he admonished himself. 'Do you need me to do anything at this auction or shall I just sit back and offer moral support?'

Tammy looked thoughtful. 'You could always auction your services for something.' Looking him straight in the eyes, she couldn't miss the twinkle of mischief that appeared in them. 'I remember you were always handy with a paint brush or roll of wallpaper,' she said, trying unsuccessfully to rein in her wayward emotions.

'I suppose I could make myself useful; it's better than just being a driver for madam.' He bowed low to emphasise his point.

'The station will appreciate any help you can give them. They're always in need of volunteers for various fundraisers.'

'Are you ready to go?' Jason replied, dangling the keys in front of her. 'Standing on the doorstep isn't getting us anywhere; we can chat and drive.' Jason held open the car door for Tammy, closing it only when he knew she was safely ensconced inside. He dashed around to the other side, quickly jumping into the driver's seat. He revved the engine and sped off.

He recalled his brief conversation with Stan, who said that Tammy helped them every year. 'So, why do you help out so much?' he asked her.

'As I said, they're always in need of volunteers and I happen to think it's a good cause.' She pressed her lips together into a thin line. 'Besides, River Springs is only a small town, and personally I think it's nice to help your neighbours out.'

'I see your point; it's a bit like that in the army. We used to help out the locals if we could with food or other things they might need. It helped not feeling as if you were fighting the enemy all the time.' Jason missed the camaraderie, but he was glad to be miles away from the war zone. 'So, what can I expect?'

Tammy smiled. 'You will have Mrs Anderson fawning all over you and plying you with food from the buffet, the way she does to all the people she likes. It is hard to say no to her; she's become a second grandmother to us.'

'Who else will I need to watch out for?'

'There's old Mr Thompson; he's an ex R.A.F pilot. He fought during World

War II. When he left the armed forces, he became a fireman. He's forever regaling us with stories of the good old days, but doesn't speak about the war much. Oh, and then there's Eric Clayton. He was a solider too, and did administrative work for the station.'

'Mr Thompson sounds like an interesting chap,' replied Jason.

'He is; he's very funny, but lonely. His children have moved out of River Springs, so he's on his own for months at a time.' Tammy's eyes would light up every time she spoke of the people who mattered to her.

'Would you ever want to leave here and explore the world?' he asked, extremely curious.

'No, I wouldn't ever want to move away from here. Though I must admit it does lack excitement at times.' Tammy dreamed of far-off sandy beaches and adventure. 'I would like to go away on holidays and such, see different places, different cultures — but I'd want to come back.'

She hadn't changed that much, then — still a home bird. Leaving certain people behind would be a wrench for her. They chatted all the way to the community centre. Even though they now sat in the car park, the easy conversation continued. Jason felt his stomach churn; being so close to Tammy resurrected all the old feelings he had for her, the ones he'd thought buried deep in his heart. Why had he let her just walk away that day? It was one of the biggest mistakes he'd made, and yet there was no way either of them could go back to simpler times.

'We'd best get inside, Tammy.' Jason stared longingly into her chocolate-brown eyes, holding her gaze far longer than he should, searching it for answers to unasked questions.

Tammy broke away first, quickly looking at her watch. 'Oh, we've been sitting here for ages.' Jumping out of the car, she nearly ran to the door of the community hall. The room had been decorated simply but tastefully. Fire helmets decorated the tables, emphasising the purpose of the fundraiser. Half the town seemed to have turned up, most of them just now being served supper.

Seeing Stan walk towards them, Jason stood at ease, shoving his hand in his pockets; what he wanted to do was grab Tammy and hold her so everyone would know she was his.

'Jason, it's good to see you again.' Stan shook Jason's hand, then held a leaflet out. 'Here's a list of all the items up for grabs in tonight's auction.'

Jason took the list and watched jealously as Stan embraced Tammy, holding her a little longer than he thought was proper. He felt out of place and extremely uncomfortable. There was history between those two and he wasn't part of it. He didn't like that feeling and gave himself a mental shake.

'You've done a grand job here Stan,' Jason said.

'I haven't done anything; all this was our Tammy and Mrs Anderson's work.'

Stan's arm was still round Tammy's shoulders and he gave her a proprietary squeeze.

'I didn't know you organised decorations as well. It looks really good, Tam,' he stuttered as she turned those dark chocolate eyes to him.

'It was a joy to do. These men mean a lot to me, so it wasn't hard.'

Stan released Tammy from his embrace. 'Tammy, stop putting yourself down,' he said. 'Why don't you two find a seat and get your supper before my boys eat it all? They're already on their second helpings.'

'Oh before I forget, Stan, Jason has offered his painting services. If anyone needs anything doing outside, he's your man.'

A huge grin appeared on Stan's face. 'Thank you, Jason. Did Tammy rope you in?'

Jason nodded. 'Something like that. She can still wrap people around her little finger, I see.' Feeling a sudden pain in his arm, he realised that Tammy had given him a playful tap. 'It is true; you did rope me in.'

'You did say you wanted to come tonight, so you can help out, since you're getting a free supper. Everyone else had to pay for a ticket,' she replied sternly.

Jason gave her a mock salute in return. 'Let's eat. I don't know about you, but the smell of food is making me hungry. I wouldn't want my free ticket to go to waste.'

'Men and their stomachs.' Stan laughed and Jason grinned.

Tammy muttered. 'I know where Toby gets it from now.'

Realising what she'd said, Tammy flicked a look at Jason. His eyebrows were pulled together in a frown. Tammy turned abruptly, heading for a table against the back wall, praying he hadn't heard her.

'Does Toby eat a lot then?' Jason asked curiously.

Damn, he did hear her. 'Yes, like a bottomless pit.'

Jason followed her lead, taking his place beside her. They sat for several minutes in companionable silence. He was pleased to see that they could have some semblance of friendship, even if at times the conversation remained strained.

Several people came up to them and commented on how pleased they were to see Tammy with such a nice young man. Tammy blushed and squirmed in her seat. She knew these people, but she was self-conscious.

Pondering all the comments, Jason guessed people weren't used to seeing her with a man, but what was up with Tammy and the firemen? They were all on first-name terms with her, and she with them.

'They seem nice,' said Jason as the last women walked away from them.

'They mean well, I suppose.' Her voice sounded tired. Tammy looked around the room. She was pleased to see so many had turned out. Mrs Anderson was doing well and had a stream of people queuing up for the raffle tickets.

Tammy thought her responsible for the idea of the calendars which had sold so quickly. She'd probably gotten the idea from the movie, *Calendar Girls*. Just the same, it was more money for the new building for ex and injured firemen.

She'd already seen Jason in his combats; what would he look like out of the uniform? Her heart rate hadn't settled since she got into his car. She could smell his musky aftershave and feel the heat resonating from his skin. A day's stubble on his face made him look even hotter than she remembered. He was close enough for her to touch, but she couldn't bring herself to do it. *He won't want you*, the nasty voice reminded her.

'Are you enjoying yourself, Tam?'

The sound of his voice pulled her back from the edge of the precipice. Her melancholy thoughts threatened to pull her down into the darkness she'd only escaped thanks to the joy Toby had brought to her. The thought of her son made her smile.

'I always enjoy these fundraisers. Stan will start the auction as soon as everyone's had their fill.'

Huffing, Jason replied, 'I haven't had mine yet.' His stomach growled in agreement.

'It will be here; honestly, I don't know who is worse, you or Toby.'

'I will take the brunt of it; after all, I am a lot older than he is.' Jason was glad they could get on without shouting or hurling insults at each other as he had seen many ex partners do. He was about to say so, when Mrs Anderson arrived at their table with a trolley.

'There you are, Jason. Tammy said you were coming. I hope you're hungry. I've given you an extra-large portion.' Mrs Anderson smiled at him as she put a heaped plate in front of him. 'Tammy, love, I've plated up some for young Toby; he asked for beans instead of mushy peas. Make sure you stop by the kitchen before you go.'

Tammy tried to stifle a giggle at the look on Jason's face. Mountains of pie and peas rose from the sea of rich, thick gravy, and the man at her side looked dismayed and amazed all at once. His stomach let out another growl, which caused Mrs Anderson to smile widely. After dishing out Tammy's plate, she moved onto the next table, and Jason groaned.

'Do I have to eat it all?'

'Oh, yes, every single morsel.' Tammy gave way to laughter, as Jason picked up his knife and fork like a man about to go into battle.

'Here I go. Wish me luck; I'm going in.'

Tammy laughed heartily at Jason's joke. They ate in companionable silence, taking in the happy atmosphere. Tammy pointed out people Jason didn't know and filled him in on their story. The Porters had moved to the town two years ago and lived just round the corner from Tammy. James

71

was a doctor and Sally worked as a nurse. The couple, desperate for a baby, had undergone three failed IVF attempts. As heart-breaking as each aborted attempt was, they'd decided to give it one last try.

Jason commented that they seemed like a happy couple. Sally looked up and smiled at her husband as he pulled out a chair for her, making sure she was comfortable. Tammy whispered that it was because she was just about 16 weeks pregnant and everything seemed to be going well for them this time.

This close-knit community was something Jason missed. After his troops had been killed, he'd lost the connection that had held him together. For the last month, he'd been floating down a river of emotion, currents deep under the surface, threatening to pull him down into the murky depths of memories he'd rather forget. He desperately needed something, someone, to hold onto; could Tammy be that person?

He finished his meal and looked

closely at the woman next to him. She seemed a world away, wistfully watching the closeness that the Porters shared. A gentle smile touched the corner of her lips, and Jason found it hard to look at her when she turned to him.

'The auction's about to start.'

'Are you bidding on anything?' Jason flicked his gaze to the table up on the stage, where Stan was standing behind a lectern.

Tammy wrinkled her nose, her shoulders rising into a shrug. 'I've had about as many cooking lessons from Mrs Anderson as she'll give me.' Admission time, she thought. 'Down at the fire house, the crews could use my sponge cake as a ramrod to break down a door in an emergency.'

Jason tried to suppress his smile, but earned a dig from her elbow for his efforts. 'What about the season ticket? Is Toby into football?'

'He likes to kick a ball around, yeah,' Tammy admitted. 'But he's a bit young to follow yet. I might have a little bid on the cinema pass; Toby loves cartoons.'

'Nothing else that takes your fancy?' Jason couldn't resist. 'Mr Rodger's gardening services? My services?' Jason's grin deepened, as he saw the blush sweep up Tammy's face.

'I-I-I don't know, I can't afford . . . ' Tammy looked everywhere except at Jason and was grateful when Stan hammered on the lectern to start the auction.

'Welcome, ladies and gentleman, boys and girls, to the first — and hopefully, not the last — River Springs Fireman and Families Fundraiser auction.' Stan's deep voice boomed around the room, amplified by the microphone. 'Sorry, folks; we'll just get the volume right!' The PA system squealed and Stan winced. 'Just checking you're all awake before we start. You might want to turn your hearing aid up, Mr Donaldson!'

The old man at the back raised his glass as the gathered crowd laughed.

'Right then, first lot is a pair of season tickets for our very own River Springs Football Club. Support our boys at every game, home and away, donated courtesy of Robert McLure, managing director. Robert is here tonight with some of the first team. How about a round of applause for River Springs FC!'

There was a huge cheer and the bidding got underway, starting slowly, but the momentum soon gathered as Stan did his best auctioneer impression. Tammy joked with Jason that one of the most popular shows in the firehouse during the afternoon was Auction Hunt, and Stan fancied himself as an amateur antique expert.

The winner of the season tickets was Dr Porter. He was an avid football fan and hoped that their firstborn was a boy. Jason could see his wife giving him a bit of a hard time, but all in jest. Dr Porter put his hand gently on her belly as he bent to kiss her; a lump came to Jason's throat seeing the tenderness between them. Would he ever have that with anyone? Would Tammy ever look at him that way?

'Next up is a cinema ticket for the year,' Stan announced loudly.

This was the lot Tammy wanted for young Toby, but on a small budget she wasn't sure she would get them.

'Who will give me £5 to start off?'

Tammy raised her hand and the crowd turned to see who had put a bid in. She prayed that no one would go beyond her £30 budget.

'£10!' a male voice shouted.

'£10 in the room any advance on £10?'

Tammy shouted '£30.'

That was it; that was all she had. If it went beyond that, Toby would have to go without something from the auction.

Looking hesitantly, she perused the room. She prayed silently that no one else would bid.

'£30 in the room. Going once at £30, going twice three times sold for £30.'

Tammy let out an audible sigh of relief; she had won the lot she wanted.

The bids came thick and fast for the next few lots. Mrs Anderson's cookery lesson was won by Mr Hamilton, owner of the garden centre. His wife had run off with the head gardener a few months earlier, and he wasn't confident in the kitchen, managing to burn even the simplest of dishes such as soup. Mrs Anderson looked thrilled to have been won.

'To think I'm worth £75, Tammy,' the older woman trilled happily as she scooped up their empty plates, 'and to Mr Hamilton.'

'Cheap at half the price, Mrs A.' Tammy was happy. She hadn't had such a good night for ages. She couldn't put her finger on it.

Jason seemed to be enjoying himself too, if his loud cheers were anything to go by.

'Our next lot is a last minute addition to the auction. As some of you may already know, our very own Corporal

Jason Rivera is home on leave, after completing several tours of duty in Afghanistan. There has been great interest in this lot. Jason is offering his services . . . '

Stan paused for effect, grinning as he got the reaction he was after — the audience gave a loud ooooo-er. 'Painting, I meant. And I have several bids from people who cannot be here this evening.'

Jason stood from his seat slightly to acknowledge the round of applause and nodded his head to Stan to start.

'Please tell me you're going to rescue me from this situation, Tam,' Jason muttered as Sheila, one of the town's most glamorous divorcees, preened and gave him a lascivious wink, looking at him from under her heavily mascaraed lashes. 'I'll be eaten alive.'

Tammy laughed with delight. 'I'd love to help you, Corporal, but you're out of my price range.' She nodded towards the stage, where Stan was reading from a piece of paper.

'I have a starting bid at £50, with the room at £50.'

'£60!' A female shouted.

'£60, I'm bid. And I have £70, £70 with me.'

Stan countered, looking round the room for bidders.

'£75.' A male voice this time, and Jason rolled his eyes.

'That's Simon; he owns the hair salon in the Square,' Tammy giggled.

'£80.'

'£80 in the room. £80, I'm bid. £90 with me. £90, £90.'

The bids kept coming, between Simon and Sheila and Stan's mystery bidder.

Jason looked bemused. He hoped that the mystery bidder would win, because Simon's enthusiasm and Sheila's ferocity were beginning to scare him. He said as much to Tammy, who scoffed. 'And there's me thinking the army was supposed to make a man of you, not a mouse,' she laughed.

The bidding slowed down at £95,

with many others who had put in single bids leaving the others to do it. Jason just wanted his part in the auction to end; after all, it was already a lot of money to pay just for some painting. He smiled wryly as he looked at Tammy as she tried to stifle a giggle. Between Simon and Sheila trying to outbid each other, the price for Jason rose to £190.

Stan looked at his bidding sheet, then pointedly around the room before he spoke. 'I have £195 with me. £195 in the room. Any advance on £195? Going once, at £195. Going twice. For £195, Corporal Rivera. Sold for £195.'

A huge cheer went up and Jason stood sheepishly, hugely relieved, and gave a salute to the crowd. Surely there was no way the mystery bidder could be as daunting as the others. He'd held out a hope that it might have been Tammy bidding anonymously through Stan, but having seen how stressed she'd been when bidding £30 for the cinema tickets for Toby, there was no way she'd have been able to hide her nerves when the money started heading over £100.

'I'm just going to call Gran and make sure that Toby's okay.' Tammy stood and Jason caught her wistful look as Stan held up a 1:20 model of a fire engine, complete with extending ladders and a siren.

'Toby would love that,' Tammy sighed. 'I won't be long. Watch out for Sheila, she'll be on the warpath. She always gets what she wants.'

Jason watched her leave the hall and then turned his attention to the bidding. He only had a few minutes. It was important to him to win the fire engine for both Tammy and Toby. The bidders were few; there had been lots of fire engine toys sold already throughout the day, and Jason won easily. He asked Stan to look after it for him until later.

The bidding was underway for the last item when Tammy took her seat. 'Oh, Mr Rodgers's gardening lot. He's such a nice man, and his garden is beautiful. Did the fire engine sell okay?' Tammy looked round the room to see who had won it.

'Some bloke got it; Toby okay with your gran?' Jason changed the subject quickly. He didn't want her to know he'd bought it for her son. She might be offended.

'Did it go for a lot?' Tammy clapped hard as the auction was concluded. 'Toby's fine. He went to bed early. Gran says he was full of talk about fire engines and the fête this afternoon.' She gave Jason a long look and grinned broadly. 'I found out who your mystery bidder is.'

'Who is it?' Jason loved to see her happy; it took him back to before, before all the loss and heartache. She'd had such a haunted look about her the last few days; it was a relief to see the tightness in her face relax.

'My mum; Gran just told me.'

Jason's mouth gaped open. 'Mrs Morgan? Why would she need me as a handyman?'

Tammy shrugged. 'Dad's not too active these days. I try and help as much as possible, but my days are filled with Toby.'

'I'll help out wherever I can,' Jason said reassuringly. 'Do you want another drink?' As he went to the bar, Jason's mind was already formulating questions he could ask Mrs Morgan, questions to which no one had given him answers — questions about Tammy, Toby, and Debbie. Yes, he'd be more than happy to help out Tammy's mum, especially if it helped him figure out what he'd missed while he'd been in Afghanistan.

'Here you go, Tammy,' he said as he returned with the drinks. 'We can get off after this if you like.' He was giving her the option, but he really didn't want to let her go yet; he was enjoying himself in her company. Out of the corner of his eye, he saw Stan approaching them carrying the fire engine. Damn, he thought; he'd asked him to give it to him later.

'Are you two enjoying yourselves?' Stan asked. 'Do you think I would make a good auctioneer?'

Jason saw Tammy's eyes open wide, seeing the fire engine tucked under Stan's arm.

'Yes, Stan you did great,' Jason told him.

Stan handed over the fire engine. 'Oh, Tammy, someone left this for you.'

'For me? Why?' Tammy stood with her mouth open.

'I assume it's for Toby, unless you like to play with toy fire engines these days.'

'Will you thank them for me?' She was lost for words. Who on earth would buy a toy at the auction and then just give it to Toby? No, he couldn't have done it; would Stan really buy a toy for Toby? He already gave them so much without this.

'Stan, you shouldn't have bought it,' Tammy chastised him.

Stan shook his head. 'No, Tammy, it wasn't me, although I will say that the bid came from someone in the room.'

Tammy looked from one man to the other and was totally bewildered. Like a streak of lightening, it hit her: Jason.

'Thank you Jason, but really you shouldn't have.'

'I didn't want you to be offended, but I guess you know me too well. I saw the way you looked at it when Stan showed the engine to the crowd, and after seeing Toby around the engines today, I knew he'd love it.'

Tammy leaned over and brushed her lips across his cheek. Jason was taken aback; it was the first sign of affection she'd shown him. *Don't read too much into it*, he cautioned himself. *She's probably just being grateful.* 'Do you want to do something else after this?' he asked her.

'With who?' Tammy's voice rose several octaves with surprise.

'Me, of course; who else did you come with?' Jason asked.

'There isn't much to do,' Tammy grumbled.

'We could go to the park and play on the swings like the old days,' Jason suggested.

Tammy covered her mouth, trying

unsuccessfully to stifle a giggle. 'Aren't we a bit old to be playing on the swings?'

'Come on; it'll be fun.' Jason tried appealing to her inner child. 'After all, children aren't supposed to be in the park after dark anyway.'

He loved the way Tammy smiled at him. Her mischievous grin told him everything he needed to know; she'd be up for a bit of fun. They needed to make their escape without being too obvious. The last thing he wanted was to start rumours about Tammy, and the River Springs grapevine worked only too well. His only plan was to make Tammy laugh on his own, without the aid of Toby or anyone else. Jason wanted her to laugh for him, to let him see a genuine smile on her face, for her to be the girl she'd been before whatever had changed her.

Tammy stood abruptly. 'I need to say good-bye to Mrs A and get Toby's food.'

'Sure, I'll meet you by the car.' Jason looked around to make sure he could escape from Sheila and Simon. Luckily, they were too busy chatting with other people to notice him heading out of the double doors. The last thing he needed was to be commandeered by Sheila and Simon, hearing them state how unfair the auction had been since they'd lost. Looking to the right of him, he saw Stan enjoying the evening air; he couldn't go without saying goodbye to him. That would have been rude; after all, he had welcomed him with open arms.

'Hey Stan, thanks for a great night. I'm going to take Tammy home,' Jason said sheepishly.

Stan nodded his head. 'Sure lad, I hope you two lovebirds enjoy yourselves.' Stan walked away whistling to himself.

Very funny, Stan, thought Jason. Too late for him to worry about his plans being passed along on the grapevine,

Jason looked at his watch. How long did it take for a woman just go and get something? He bet Tammy was standing there talking with that nice Mrs Anderson. He bet himself a drink that Tammy would say she got held up chatting — so much for a quick getaway.

Jason stood by the car tapping his foot, checking his watch for the umpteenth time in as many minutes. He and Tammy seemed to have reached a quiet peace; he was glad that after a few hours together, she had relaxed a bit more with him.

'Come on then, I'm ready.' Tammy had appeared out of nowhere, her arms laden with the fire engine and two containers of food. 'Sorry, I got held up.'

'Chatting with Mrs Anderson?' Jason asked smugly.

'Erm, yes, how did you guess?'

Jason loved the look of confusion on Tammy's face, like the time she had thought Spain was the capital of

France. The way she'd knit her brow. 'I owe myself a drink,' he said.

'What do you mean, you owe yourself a drink?' Tammy gave him a dig in the ribs, just like the old days — the second he had earned in as many hours.

'I told myself that you would be happily chatting away, whilst I waited around outside like an idiot.'

'Is my soldier boy getting impatient?' Tammy laughed heartily for the first time in a long time.

'Are you ready to go my lady, or do you want to find someone other than me to chat with?' Jason feigned he was slightly annoyed that she was taking the mickey out of him. He would find a way of getting back at her when she least expected it as he done before. Now, this felt more like the old days. Tammy seemed to be getting happier as the night wore on.

'Do you want to put the stuff in the boot?' he asked, looking in her hands and seeing the two containers. 'Toby sure eats a lot,' he commented.

'One of them is for you. Mrs Anderson thinks you need fattening up a bit.' She looked him up and down, and she personally liked the way he looked. He was lean and muscular — everything she wanted in a man, even if her head told her otherwise. They talked non-stop all the way to the park.

'What was it like out there, in Afghanistan?'

'The heat was a major problem as we're not used to it. A lot of the lads became dehydrated and ill with sun-stroke.' He smiled. 'We even had a fast food mess tent selling burgers and chips. I tell you, that was way popular with everyone. Spending nights in battle holes with the other soldiers built up a camaraderie I haven't seen before.' He paused before continuing. 'We even slept six to a tent, but we all had our own space, and nets over our bunks to keep out the bugs.'

'You're serious? A fast food place?' To Tammy it all seemed so unreal. And she couldn't believe what they were going to do. Weren't they a bit old to be sneaking in at night and playing on the swings and the slide? She was twenty-four years old, not a baby anymore. 'So, are you going to tell me why you've decided we need to play around like we're a couple of kids?'

She saw Jason's huge grin in the rear view mirror. Her heart skipped a beat, as he looked more handsome than ever when he smiled.

'Because I think we both need to let our hair down,' he replied evenly.

'Well, you don't have any hair to let down,' she quipped.

Tammy loved his army-style haircut and was in no hurry to see him change it. Even though it would grow in again, she never wanted him to have it longer. Tammy would be quite happy to see him every day wearing his army gear. Checking herself, Tammy couldn't believe she was thinking like that — as if Jason would ever listen to her about the style of his clothes or the way he wore his hair. They weren't even together anymore.

They parked on the road. Jumping out of the car, they scouted the area, looking for the groundsman. The gates to the park were always left open. It was a bit of fun; the groundsman knew people used the park after dark, but as long as no damage was done, he was fine with it; however, if he caught you, then he'd make you come back during the day to buy him a drink. Mr Taylor was a nice old man and had looked after the park for as long as Jason and Tammy could remember. Tammy knew he must have caught a lot of people last winter with deep snow. She was almost positive that adults would have sneaked in to ride down the devil's bumps on their children's sleighs.

The happy couple took one last look around and walked by the line of conifers onto the gravel walkway, keeping their eyes peeled. The moon shone brightly. The park was deserted, but the gate had been left wide open.

Tammy thought that was unusual, since the gate was generally shut. Most people knew that although the gate was on the latch, it wasn't locked, unless of course it was padlocked.

'I'll bet I can beat you off the jump,' Jason shouted as he ran to the swings like a child running down the stairs on Christmas morning. He couldn't remember the last time they had gone to the park and done this, reliving their childhood.

Tammy looked at him as he ran. It was strange the way his ankle wasn't healing as well as it should. Jason had told her he had only twisted it, and an injury like that would usually heal pretty quickly. Tammy chased after him; she felt like they were back in high school again.

Jason was already trying to go as high as possible before she'd even gotten to the swing.

'You're cheating!' Tammy shouted breathlessly.

'Nope, all is fair in love and beating

you.' Jason chuckled.

Jumping on swing next to him, she pumped her legs until she matched his pace. 'Ready, Jason? One, two . . . ' Before she could say three, Jason jumped and had landed awkwardly on the ground. Tammy tried jumping off, but she was laughing too hard and just slid straight off.

'I win!' Jason shouted and punched the air.

'That was cheating! I was laughing at you too much; I couldn't concentrate on my own jump.' It took a few minutes before Tammy conceded defeat. 'Come on, we best go before Mr Taylor catches us.'

'Too late, young uns,' a gruff voice replied.

Tammy looked up and saw Mr Taylor standing in front of them. 'It looks like we owe you a drink,' Tammy replied.

'Nah, you don't, lassy, but your boyfriend does for cheating,' he said whilst pointing a stick towards Jason. 'I was watching you the whole time. It's amazing how many people I've caught since they installed CCTV.'

Tammy and Jason looked at each other and smiled. 'Who's cheating now, Mr Taylor?'

'Since when did the park get CCTV?' Jason enquired, raising his eyebrow slightly.

'Ah, it must be several years now since we had it installed. The council was worried about the vandals in our park.' Mr Taylor waved his arm around, emphasising his point.

'Why would anyone want to ruin the park?' Tammy asked.

'Kids get bored easily these days. Not much for them to do.' He sighed heavily before he continued. 'You best keep my secret; I like getting me drinks.'

'We promise we won't tell a soul,' they replied in unison.

Waving good-bye to Mr Taylor, they turned and slowly made their way back to the car. 'Can you believe the audacity of him?' Jason said.

'Come on Jason, it's only a bit of fun.

Since his wife died, catching people playing in the park at night has been like a hobby to him, especially as the ones he does catch are adults like us, playing on the swings or balance beams.'

'I suppose so, but I still say he cheated worse than I did.' Jason folded his arms across his chest.

'Oh, stop being a baby,' Tammy chided him. With his arms folded like that he looked just like a petulant child. Tammy wanted to stand him on the naughty step to make him realise how silly he was being. They had been playing a game; just this time Mr Taylor had played it better than they had.

They walked in silence back to the car as Jason continued to sulk. He hated being beaten by anybody, least of all a groundskeeper with a spare set of eyes, watching and just waiting to pounce. Tammy could feel the awkwardness in the car; the air was tense as the electricity arced between them.

Jason stopped reluctantly outside

Tammy's house; he didn't want to let her go. Not just yet. He was having as good a time as she seemed to be. After all the tension in the restaurant and then earlier in the day at the fundraiser, it seemed for the first time since she'd seen him, Tammy had managed to relax around him. Jason was hoping it would continue, unless she decided to put those barriers up again.

He handed her the things from the car and stood just inches away. Tammy could feel his hot breath on her face. Taking a step back, she took the things from him. Her whole body tingled in anticipation whilst her stomach twisted into knots. She could feel the heat on her face; her body shook with nervous anticipation of what she hoped would come.

Finally, Jason broke the spell. 'I'm doing your mum's painting tomorrow.'

'Right, do a good job for them,' Tammy replied nonchalantly. 'Goodbye Jason, I had a good time tonight.' With that, Tammy turned and escaped into the house.

Jason stood for several minutes before getting back in the car. He had wanted to lean towards her and brush his lips against hers, but that wouldn't have done. Tammy had run a mile as it was; it was obvious she had wanted to get away from him as quickly as possible.

Tammy stood behind the front door breathing heavily, her heart threatening its escape as it beat hard against her chest. The voice in her head mocked her: *Well, what did you expect?* A single tear trickled down her face as she fought to control her emotions. Tammy wished things were different and not as confusing. Life had the habit of getting in the way. Things had been so much simpler as a child; after all, what did you need to do except go to school and play with your friends? Tammy almost wished she were a child again; at least that way, Debbie would still be with her.

4

Jason arrived at Mrs Morgan's house bright and early the next morning. He hadn't made any other plans for the day since it would take several hours to paint the fence. He couldn't help but wonder how he had let himself get roped into this.

First, there'd been the auctioning of his services; he wouldn't have turned Tammy down. Now, Tammy's mother had him painting at her house. Turning Tammy down would only have made her even more annoyed with him. Jason felt he couldn't do much right in Tammy's eyes, despite the fact that they'd had a good time the previous night.

He'd bought the fire engine for Toby, and even that had gotten disapproving looks from her. Tammy had gazed so wistfully at the engine; he'd just known she'd wanted it for the little boy. Jason had realised early in the night that she couldn't afford it, and she'd have been too proud to have accepted money from him to allow her to bid on it. He had tried to get her to bid on him, but just the way she had reacted had told him there had been no chance of that.

Now, because of that, he stood waiting around outside her parents' house. It was ironic; Mrs Morgan wasn't too proud to pay for help, but her daughter refused anything at all. It was a good job; he enjoyed working outside after all the time he'd spent in the boiling, dusty desert. The weather was surprisingly good for autumn. The sun shone brightly in the sky and the breeze blew so slightly that it wasn't enough to even dry the washing.

Jason looked at the roses which lined the garden fence; he remembered how they had been the talk of the street. Now, they wilted in the sun; the fragrant scent had vanished. Many of the paving slabs on the driveway were cracked and in desperate need of replacing. If he remembered correctly, Mr Morgan had won several awards for his garden. He'd been so proud of it. Jason remembered he used to jump over the little garden wall and the rose bushes. He chuckled to himself as he remembered how Mr Morgan would yell, 'Watch my roses!' It had never stopped him, and he had to admit he had thought of doing it when he pulled up, but that wouldn't have been any fun. There was no risk of him damaging the roses — not that he ever did or would.

Jason had no idea what had happened since he'd been away. The whole family seemed to have changed and whatever it was, they were keeping it to themselves. The paint on the windows was peeling and looked a state. If the front garden and the rose bushes were anything to go by, he dreaded to think what else needed to be done. He knocked on the door and waited patiently. Mrs Morgan appeared, wearing a pair of yellow marigolds and an apron. A small amount of flour decorated her face. Jason smiled; it was an endearing sight. He'd missed this, seeing his own mum covered in flour and the taste of her home cooking. Life wasn't the same out in the desert; the food was sufficient and they'd improved the quality of it in the last few years, but finding grains of sand in everything you ate made it less appetizing.

'Hi, Mrs Morgan; I'm here to fulfil my duty,' he said, flashing his most dazzling smile.

'I've left the painting things outside for you, Jason.' A half smile crossed her mouth. 'Come through and you can get started, unless you'd like a drink first?'

'No, it's fine,' Jason replied. 'I'd best get started; no idea how long this weather is going to last.' He wanted to keep busy — do anything other than think about his friends, of his patrol, and why he hadn't done anything to help. He should have been more watchful, paid more attention to the warning signs. Now they were all dead, and it was his fault.

He could still hear their cries in his dreams when or if he eventually fell asleep. More often than not, he would wake up screaming, beads of sweat covering his brow. He didn't want to close his eyes and relive the horror he'd faced. He drank gallons of coffee each day to try and stay awake. The doctors had said that the dreams would get easier and fade in time, possibly to the point where he would forget altogether. How would he ever forget what he had done? They had no idea what he was going through. Did they truly believe a bottle of tablets would fix everything and make his guilt go away?

Jason put on the overalls Mrs Morgan had supplied and started painting the fence. It was therapeutic to see something he'd done make the garden look so much better. Looking around, Jason spotted several other things which needed doing. The small garden wall was in desperate need of repointing. There were numerous clumps of weeds growing around the Stargazer rose bushes, and the garden shed could use a lick of paint. The grass was in desperate need of feeding and watering, and most of the plants which once bloomed in a rainbow of colour were dying.

Maybe he could ask if they had other jobs he could do. He wouldn't charge, of course — well, maybe a nice cup of tea for his toil and some of Mrs Morgan's famous fruit cake. He remembered the conversation he'd had with Tammy. Her father had lost interest in a lot of things. Jason felt badly; he'd always like the Morgans. He would keep to his word and help out in any way he could.

Several hours later, the fence looked as good as new. That should last a few more years, he thought, pleased with himself for the work. Looking at the remaining paint, he knew there was enough to do the garden shed, so he wandered over and started on that. Two jobs for the price of one! A wry smile crossed his lips.

An eerie quiet had descended over the Morgan house. Mrs Morgan had the same haunted look in her eyes that Tammy did — maybe not as pronounced, but something had gone terribly wrong in the family, and no one seemed to want to discuss it.

A police helicopter flew overhead, intruding in to his private thoughts. It was a welcome distraction; it made him wonder for whom they were searching. Was it a car they were chasing, or did they have a burglar on the run? Jason continued to pass his time working, and while it might not be the most amusing thing to do, it stopped him thinking melancholy thoughts about Tammy and her family.

'You've done a grand job of the garden fence, Jason.' Mrs Morgan brought her hands to her face, a look of sheer disbelief etched onto it. 'Oh my goodness, you've even painted the shed.'

Jason shrugged his shoulders; it hadn't been a difficult job, and he'd loved working outside. 'It's no problem, Mrs Morgan, honestly,' he tried to reassure her. 'I'm happy I could help, and auctioning my services was all for a good cause.' He kicked the paint canister. 'There was enough paint left over so I thought I might as well do the shed too.'

'Our Tammy didn't have to convince you just a little bit, Jason?'

He couldn't mistake the tone in her voice. 'Well, maybe she did a little persuading,' he admitted. 'I saw a few other things that could do with a bit of TLC.' Jason waved his hands around. 'Your little garden wall needs repointing and the weeds around the roses should be pulled.' Jason didn't like the sad way the roses looked. 'If you'd like, I can come back over the next few days and finish things off.' He stood to attention whilst he waited for a reply.

'I would appreciate that. Mr Morgan has let things go over the last few years.' Mrs Morgan gestured towards the house. 'But surely you have better things to do with your time than waste it doing odd jobs for me?'

'No, I don't have anything on. In fact, I'm on leave for quite a while.' He paused. 'I want to be kept busy; I can't bear to be idle.' At least he was telling the truth. Well, partly, since he didn't know if his leave would become permanent.

'After all your hard work, why don't you come in and have a nice bowl of homemade stew to warm you up?'

Jason's stomach growled in appreciation; he didn't need to be asked a second time. He had worked up an appetite. Mrs Morgan showed him the way to the dining room. He chuckled to himself — as if he could have forgotten the way after all the time he'd spent here in the past.

The room hadn't changed much. The large oak dresser still stood against the far wall, lacy doilies protecting the polished surface. It was cluttered with bone china plates and cups with a bright rose painted on each of them. Several pictures of Tammy and Toby adorned the walls. There was one that he couldn't make out clearly, but the reed cross attached to the picture, the sort you got on Palm Sunday, had the letters R.I.P. painted in black letters across it. Jason's curiosity was piqued, but he didn't have a chance to investigate further. Mrs Morgan came in carrying a tray with his stew and bread rolls.

'Sit down dear, and get your dinner whilst it's nice and hot.' Her motherly manner showed itself. He was hard pressed to decide whose cooking he enjoyed more, his mother's or Mrs Morgan's. After finishing the hearty meal, Jason stood and wandered over to the picture to examine it more closely. It was a photograph of Tammy and Debbie sitting in the garden. It looked like it had been a summer's day, but

Tammy had a large quilt wrapped around her.

That was strange. It looked like it was a hot day, so why would Tammy have been wrapped in a quilt? Unless, of course, she had been ill; perhaps that was the reason. Above the 'rest in peace' on the cross was Debbie's name. Jason felt the tears prick the backs of his eyes. Now he knew what Tammy had meant when she'd said Debbie wasn't here anymore.

Why hadn't Tammy said anything to him? How his comments must have hurt her. He'd continued to insist that she tell him where Debbie was. He could only assume that she'd thought he didn't care — hadn't cared about what had happened to her after he'd left. Jason hadn't wanted to break up with her, but seeing how adamant Tammy had been, he'd let her go without a fight, saying it was best not to keep in contact. He had cut Debbie out of his life too. Jason hadn't wanted Tammy to think he would move on to her cousin, even though it was nothing like that.

'I've brought you some cake, Jason.' Mrs Morgan interrupted his thoughts.

'Honestly, I couldn't eat another thing, Mrs Morgan.' He couldn't eat another thing if he tried; he felt sick to his stomach. Debbie was dead and Tammy had hid it from him; what sort of person was she?

'What happened to Debbie?' He needed to know, *had* to know what had happened to his friend. He couldn't understand why nobody had told him about it. It must have happened whilst he was away; surely someone could have phoned him or written him a letter to tell him. They wouldn't have given him leave as Debbie wasn't a relative, but at least he would have known.

'Didn't Tammy tell you, Jason?' The sympathetic tone in her voice was unmistakable.

Jason shook his head. 'No. She hasn't told me anything.'

'Sit down, Jason,' Mrs Morgan

replied, pointing to the chairs.

Jason did as he was told, waiting for whatever bad news was going to come. Tammy would have a lot of explaining to do when he got hold of her.

Mrs Morgan waited until she thought Jason was listening before beginning her sorry tale. 'When you and Tammy split up, just before you left for the army I believe it was, she was inconsolable. Debbie suggested that Tammy move in with her.'

She caught him fidgeting in his chair and twirling the teaspoon around in his fingers. 'The photograph you just saw was the last one taken of the girls. My niece was always a vivacious child.'

Taking a tissue out of her pocket, she dabbed her eyes. 'It happened a few days after that picture was taken. They had been out late that night and had come home tired and hungry. Debbie went off upstairs to change, and Tammy went to put the chip pan on and settled down in the front room.'

Mrs Morgan saw that Jason looked

uneasy, as if he knew what was coming next. 'Both girls had become very tired; I can only assume that Tammy fell asleep in the living room, as we believe that is what Debbie did.' Mrs Morgan paused to allow this piece of information to sink in, and so she could breathe herself.

'When Tammy woke, the house was ablaze. Luckily, the fire brigade came quickly and a fireman got our Tammy out, while another man went for Debbie.' It was hard for her to relive the horrors of her family's loss. 'Debbie passed away the next day in hospital. They think she was overcome with smoke.'

For a moment Mrs Morgan found it difficult to carry on. Jason just stayed still and waited until she felt able to continue. 'During the investigation they found some poisonous substances, possibly from the ceiling tiles in the girls' bedroom; Tammy suffered severe burns down her arm and partway onto her chest as she tried to escape the flames.'

'Those hideous cardigans she wears,' mumbled Jason. It explained so much — and then again, so little. He was angry that no one had told him about Debbie, unless they thought he'd had no right to know.

'Her father and I believe that Tammy has blamed herself all these years for the accident; and that's what it was, a horrific accident.'

Jason didn't miss the emphasis she'd placed on the word accident.

'When Debbie died, part of Tammy died with her; Toby was born that night in hospital. The shock from the fire induced early labour.'

Jason sat in silence for several minutes trying to process what he had just been told. 'Where's Toby's dad?' Debbie was gone, and a little boy who somehow managed to stay alive? It was a question that would stick in his mind and haunt him.

'Tammy's never said who Toby's father was. We have an idea, but I wouldn't want to point the finger at an innocent young man.'

Of course, Tammy would know who the father of her friend's child would be. After all, they used to confide in each other all the time. The two girls were forever huddled in some corner or other, whispering. 'I suppose that's fair enough. It's a shame for Toby to grow up without both parents.'

'Mm,' was all the reply Mrs Morgan gave him.

That was strange; why was Mrs Morgan so evasive? Maybe what she had said was right, and they didn't know who the father was. Something was still bothering him, but no matter how hard he tried, he couldn't put his finger on it. He didn't like to be out of the loop if he could help it. He supposed that it was the soldier in him.

'Thank you for telling me, Mrs Morgan, and I'm so sorry about Debbie.' Jason saw the hurt on her face, the pain still raw for all the family. He shouldn't get involved; he had enough of his own problems to deal with without dealing with someone else's.

Maybe he could just help Tammy regain a little bit of self-esteem whilst he was on leave. Now he understood why they'd let things go. Everyone was still grieving for Debbie, but he knew better than most that you have to carry on with living. Jason thought maybe a grief counsellor would help her to deal with all her problems, providing she'd even see one. Or maybe a bit of gentle persuasion from her friend Stan would do the trick. He'd come home to deal with his own problems; now he'd deal with someone else's, too.

'That's okay, Jason. We all just take it one day at a time; it seems a little cliche, but that's what you have to do.' Drying her eyes, she attempted a smile, but it wouldn't come. 'I'm more than happy to have you finish those jobs you mentioned. I'll pay you of course.'

He waved his hands in front of him. 'No, there's no need; I'm not doing it for money. You have always been good to me, and this is my way of repaying your kindness.'

'OK, if that is how you want it.' She never won when she argued with Jason. 'Would you take one of my fruit cakes then, as payment?'

Jason rose from his seat. 'Now you are talking.' He gave her his cheekiest grin. 'I would do anything for some of your fruit cake.' He winked at her. 'I'd better get going. Thank you for the lovely dinner.'

She nodded. 'Jason, try and make our Tammy happy again. I know how much she has missed you.'

He didn't answer. Jason wandered over, kissed her on the cheek, and made his way to the front door. He was covered in paint and desperately needed a shower. Why would Mrs Morgan ask him that? How could he make Tammy happy again when they weren't even what he could call friends? Wasn't it her idea to break up with him? He could still be making her happy if she hadn't decided to let him go.

As he was driving home, he felt an overwhelming desire to see Tammy. He wanted to tell her that he knew what had happened. Maybe talking to an old friend would help. No! Why on earth would she want to discuss anything with an ex? It had been a long time since they'd been friends. Even if Tammy felt she couldn't talk to him, at least she'd know he'd be there if she ever did need someone. But he couldn't go round looking like this; he was a complete mess. Perhaps he should leave it until tomorrow. Mrs Morgan had given him a lot to think about and he knew he needed space and time to think and mull things over. The last thing Tammy needed was him jumping on her, demanding that she let him help her.

Tammy had always been so independent, so in charge, and he'd loved that about her. If anyone had needed any organising, whether it was for a party or just their wardrobe, every one of their friends had called Tammy. Even at school, she'd been the one who never forgot to write down what homework had to be done, and she'd make sure they even handed it in on time.

Those were the days, he thought sadly. They'd been young, carefree, and the world had been their playground. Now, responsibilities and families had taken over — except in Tammy's case, she didn't just have responsibilities; she carried around the heavy chain of guilt, guilt that no one else had hung around her neck. She'd done that herself. He knew how that felt because the burden she carried was the same one he did.

Tammy wouldn't accept help readily; she never had. She didn't want to be seen as a charity case. Not that anyone thought that, but she was proud of who she was and felt she was the one who needed to take charge and help other people, not the other way around.

Would she allow him to help her? That was the big question. Could he do anything? Tomorrow he was determined to find out. He wouldn't ring; a surprise visit would be better. If she wasn't in, he'd just try again later. He wouldn't let Tammy give him some lame excuse as to why he couldn't come round, or give her a chance to ignore the phone. She was unlikely to ignore the front door. *Be patient, Jason.* Tomorrow would come soon enough.

5

Tammy stood in the kitchen, preparing a picnic for herself and Toby. Whenever the weather was nice, she always tried to go to the park for a picnic. She loved to spend quality time with her son, and it allowed him to burn off some energy. These were the days she didn't worry about rushing to get him to nursery or going off to the shops.

It had only been two days since she'd seen Jason, but already it felt like years. As she looked around, she noticed that her normally tidy kitchen looked like a building site. Packing the last of the containers into her bag, Tammy set about righting her kitchen, so that it looked at least halfway normal. She hated having anything out of its proper place, but she wouldn't have time to give it the deep cleaning she knew it needed. Tammy chuckled; some people wouldn't agree. Her kitchen was never mucky, but cleaning provided a release from all her problems.

A loud knock on the door interrupted her chores. She walked through the hallway, realising she still held the cleaning cloth in her hand. She shrugged her shoulders and turned the lock on the heavy oak door.

'Jason! I didn't expect to see you.' Tammy struggled to reign in her emotions.

'I was just passing by and thought I'd stop and see you.' Jason looked at the cloth in her hand. 'I'm sorry; have I interrupted you?'

She detected the apologetic tone of his voice. 'I was just getting ready to go to the park. Do you want to come in for a minute?' Tammy moved away from the door to allow him access if he wanted it.

Jason stepped quickly inside, lest Tammy change her mind. He'd found it hard to stay away, especially now that he knew how much grief she carried around with her. He wanted to be there to love and comfort her. No, not to love — he couldn't love anyone; he didn't deserve that.

'Where did you say you were going?' he asked, trying to sound as casual as possible.

'I'm only going to the park with Toby for a picnic,' Tammy said as she took Jason into the kitchen. 'I try and take him every weekend; afterwards, he spends the night over at Mum and Dad's house.'

His head snapped up. 'You'll be on your own tonight? Do you fancy doing something later?' he asked hesitantly.

Tammy's heart skipped a beat, and for once she managed to ignore the nagging voice in her head. 'I'd like that,' she answered shyly. 'If you aren't busy, why don't you join us in the park?' The words rushed out before she had a chance to think things through.

'I'm not busy; where is the little man?' Jason asked.

'I left him in the front room,

watching cartoons.'

Jason watched as she grabbed two cups out of the cupboard. 'Do you want a cup of tea before we go?'

'No, I'm fine; do you want me to go and sit with him until you're ready?' There was a catch in his voice. The last thing he needed was to push Tammy too far; it was possible she'd run a mile in the opposite direction.

Tammy showed him into the front room. 'Toby, could you watch Jason for me, please?'

'Yes mummy; he can watch cartoons with me,' replied Toby, patting the settee next to him before turning his eyes back to the television screen.

Jason complied and sat down beside Toby, whose eyes were glued to the screen. The boy didn't seem to mind strangers. Wasn't that unusual for a child that age? Weren't they normally wary of people they didn't know? Jason put it down to the fact that he spent so much time at the fire station that he wasn't as shy as other children his age.

'What are we watching?' he asked, trying to make conversation.

Toby smiled. '*Duck Tales*. They go on adventures'

'Do you like adventures?' Jason asked curiously.

'Yes. Mummy's boring; she doesn't like exciting things.'

Jason chuckled; Toby sounded like an old man rather than a child of four. 'Well, that's mummies for you.'

Toby leaned against him and settled back down to watch his programme; Jason found it extremely comforting that the boy felt he made a useful cushion. He didn't think he was much good for anything else.

Tammy re-entered the room quietly and saw her little man snuggled on the sofa with Jason, both totally oblivious to her presence. If she wandered to the armchair she would have alerted them to her presence, so she stood still, letting them finish watching the episode. She remembered viewing the same cartoon when she'd been younger. When the final credits rolled, she coughed slightly to garner their attention.

'How long have you been standing there, Tam?'

Tammy caught the look of embarrassment etched on his face. 'Long enough! Enjoy the cartoon, did you?' Tammy laughed aloud. She loved the fact that she'd caught Jason enjoying something as simple as a cartoon; he sat there looking like a naughty teenager again. No doubt he'd get his own back; she could never do anything without him repaying her in kind. Warmth swam through her veins, a feeling she'd missed.

'I'm ready to go if you two are,' Jason said.

'Mummy, we're watching cartoons,' Toby pouted.

'Hey Toby, we can always watch cartoons another day.' Jason held out his hand. 'I think your mummy wants to go and play on the swings.' He winked at her.

'Oh, okay then.' Toby jumped up and rushed to the door.

'You certainly have a way with kids.' A pang of jealousy hit her. Jason had done the trick; Toby would've had a temper tantrum if she'd tried to drag him out of the house and away from his favourite cartoon. But she would take him to the park on the same day the TV Channel was having a *Duck Tales* marathon.

Tammy didn't want Toby to get too close to Jason. How would her little boy cope once Jason went back overseas? The last thing she wanted was to hurt her son, but she was torn. She couldn't allow herself to love Jason; it wasn't fair to him. She'd just have to try and cope with the myriad emotions she was feeling. She needed to lock them away again, deep inside her heart. Tammy knew she would have to push Jason away again, though she didn't like doing the opposite of what she really wanted to do.

'Where are we off to, Madam?' Jason

asked, interrupting her musing.

'Just quit it with the 'madam' bit,' she said testily. 'We're off to Springston Hall. They've built a better park there; it even has picnic tables.'

'I remember we went there on our first date. Didn't they have some sort of fair going on on the grounds?'

Tammy swallowed and couldn't help but notice the faraway look in his eye. 'Yes, but they've only done it a few times since then.' She held out the picnic hamper to him. 'Here. If you're going to tag along, you can make yourself useful.'

Toby laughed as Jason saluted her. He grabbed the boy's hand and steered him outside to his car. 'Do you go to the park a lot Toby?' he asked.

Toby rolled his eyes. 'All the time!'

Jason laughed heartily. 'How about a game of hide-and-seek around the memorial statue?'

'How do you know about the stone people?' Toby asked, wrinkling his brow.

Toby's puzzled face made Jason

smile. 'I used to play the same game with my mummy and daddy at your age,' he answered and grinned.

'Oh, okay.' Toby's reply was noncommittal.

'Aren't you too old for something like that, Jason?' Tammy smirked as she remembered all the times they had played hide-and-seek around the same statue, well into their teenage years. They'd run all over the park, hiding and climbing the trees in the woodland areas.

'Let me tell you something, Ms Morgan. You are never too old for a good game of hide and seek; it works up an appetite.'

'Well, you definitely don't need any help in that department. From what I remember, you're always hungry,' she countered.

'Some things never change, so I hope you brought a lot to eat.' Jason roared with laughter.

Tammy was glad that things were okay between them. At least they could laugh and joke the way they had in the old days. Having a man to play games with instead of just his mother would make it more fun for Toby.

'Do you mind if we take my car? Toby's child seat is fixed in,' Tammy asked.

'No, that's fine; we'll take yours now, and if you're still up for dinner later, we can go in mine.'

'Erm, sure Jason,' she replied as the hairs on the back of her neck stood on end, and a tingling sensation swept through her body.

She was going on a date with Jason! What would she wear? *Tammy, you really shouldn't do this*, cried the stupid voice in her head. 'Just shut up!' she said.

'What do you mean, shut up?' replied Jason.

'Sorry! I didn't realise I'd said that out loud.' Tammy felt the heat on her face. 'I was just having a conversation with myself.' Now she sounded as though she was totally nuts. *Great.*

What must he think of me?

Jason smiled. 'Don't worry. Come on, let's get going, hun.' Oops! Hopefully his slip wouldn't be noticed. Hadn't he promised himself to stay away from women? He was being inexplicably drawn to Tammy. He wanted to help her try and see that things hadn't been her fault. *Don't be stupid; how can you protect her when you couldn't protect your squad?* That thought pounded into his heart like a dagger, trying to put gloom on the proceedings, but he shook it off.

They drove in silence to the park. The old mansion stood majestically at the top of a gravel path surrounded by acres of woodland and cultivated gardens. It had always taken Tammy's breath away, even though it was over five hundred years old. They had both visited it often during various times in their lives. When Tammy was a child, Jason remembered she learnt to ride her bike on the grounds; and as a teenager, she'd come to see him on his dinner breaks.

There was a café for the visitors that had appeared in a well-known film from the early 60's, although for the life of her, Tammy couldn't remember its title. She hated the fact that she couldn't remember the name, as it would annoy her until she did. Some people came here just so that they could say they'd eaten at the same café.

The three of them made their way over to the memorial statue and placed a picnic rug and their hamper on the ground.

'Right, who wants to play hide-and-seek now? Or do you both want to eat first?' Jason enquired.

Tammy waited for Toby's answer. 'Play first, mummy!' he cried as he jumped up and down on the spot.

'Ok, I'll count to twenty. You and Jason go and hide; the first person I catch has to count, okay?' Tammy said with authority. She turned around and climbed the three small steps to the memorial; her view would be totally obscured, and it would allow Toby to hide behind the wall or the conifers which lined the paths surrounding the statue. Counting as slowly and as loudly as she could, she gave them a few more seconds and shouted, 'Ready or not!'

Toby usually hid behind the wall, as it was much easier for him not to be seen. Many times Tammy pretended she couldn't see him just to prolong the game. She decided to find Jason first. Toby hated being the one to seek people, but he loved to hide. The huge smile he wore on his face when he hadn't been found until the end was priceless.

Walking around the rows of conifers and seeing nothing, she knew the only other place they could be hiding was in Toby's favourite spot. Tammy smiled to herself. Instead of going around the wall, she walked along its top. Jason was face-down in the dirt.

'Found you, Jason,' Tammy said as

she stood towering over him. 'You're on.'

Toby came out of his hiding place and ran to grab Tammy's hand. A sudden gush of wind made Tammy shiver. It wasn't the best of days, although the sky was aquamarine with a scattering of cotton wool clouds.

'That was cheating, Tammy, and you know it.'

'No, Jason; I knew standing up there, I'd be able to see behind the wall.' She laughed.

Taking up his position by the statue, Jason started to count as Tammy had done, but he hadn't closed his eyes.

As he stared at the statue before him, his vision blurred until everything meshed into one. The three statues were a monument to all those who'd lost their lives in the two great wars. He couldn't move, unable to take his eyes from the statue. He wasn't sure how long he'd stood there; was it a few seconds, or hours? It had gone eerily quiet except for the wind rustling through the trees, shaking the leaves off their branches.

The noises started — the machine-gun fire and bombs exploding all around him. He could hear their cries and screams for help, but all he could do was lie there and watch. He'd tried to crawl to them, but something had held him back, pushing searing pain into his leg. He couldn't move. Seeing the black box, he'd reached for it without waiting for the pain to subside, and used the radio to call for help. He lost consciousness. The next thing he remembered, he lay on a bed in the hospital tent.

Jason's eyes glazed over with unshed tears for his fallen comrades.

Tammy watched as Jason continued to stand motionless, staring at the statue, his fists clenched and held stiffly by his sides. She'd never seen him like this before and had no idea what had put him in such a state. Had his ghosts come back, or was he paying silent tribute to the men from the great wars?

She walked slowly towards him, almost tiptoeing, scared to make a noise. When she finally faced him, she saw the look of pure horror in his eyes as a solitary tear ran down his cheek. She lifted her hand and wiped it away.

'Jason, are you all right?' She moved forward hesitantly and encircled him with her arms; her heart ached for him. She'd never seen him so upset. When they'd gone their separate ways he hadn't looked sad and depressed. At least, not that he had shown her how he felt, or even told her; Jason had just let her walk out of his life.

Standing on tip-toes, she brushed her lips against his, wanting the kiss to bring him out of himself. He responded hungrily, claiming her mouth, holding her tightly in his embrace. For that one moment, no one else existed; it was just the two of them in their own world — no troubles to hurt them, no one to disturb them. When they finally came up for air, Tammy realised what she had done.

'I'm so sorry Jason, I . . . ' but she couldn't find the words. She turned to walk away, but he held her back. The flames of passion Tammy thought she had buried long ago stirred, reigniting the embers. Just looking up at him now, she knew with absolute clarity that she loved him as much now as she ever did. Why on earth had she let him go? Pretending to everyone that she hated him, when the reality was she knew that she could never be with anyone other than Jason. The only person Tammy really hated was herself. All the great ideas of being horrible to him were being thrown out of the window. The truth needed to come out. They both hid dark secrets, and hers would tear him apart.

'Don't go, and don't say you're sorry,' he whispered, sadness etching his voice. Jason wasn't sorry. He'd missed the way Tammy felt against him. Missed the silly tricks and long conversations they used to have. He missed everything about her, but

Tammy had decided she no longer wanted him. Perhaps she had outgrown him. He had never known the reason, but he still missed and loved her. He tilted her head to his and gave her one last lingering kiss — knowing that to kiss her again would put their tentative friendship on the line.

Tammy stared at him. She didn't like how her body still responded to his touch. She needed a change of subject, and quick, before she was tempted again. 'Won't you tell me about it? What's wrong Jason? You look so sad.' Jason liked how she was still stroking his arm, even if she didn't realise she was doing it.

'Why don't we sit down and I'll tell you. It isn't a nice tale; I don't want to upset you.' Jason was relieved to finally tell someone; he'd harboured these feelings of regret and terror since it had happened. He couldn't talk to his parents about it. Tammy seemed the only one he could ever tell the horrors of his life to.

'Toby, come and get your dinner!' Tammy shouted.

Running out of his hiding spot, he joined them on the rug.

'I'm just going to go over to the statue with Jason. Stay here where we can still see you,' she said firmly.

Tammy wandered back over to the statue and sat on the wall, watching as Jason paced up and down. Her heart ached to see him so unhappy and listless. She would have done anything to take his pain away — even wishing that the pain she had caused could be magicked away. Pity there weren't any real fairy godmothers to make that happen.

'I'm not on leave Tammy; the army sent me home. They said I was not fit to continue active duty.' The confusion on her face was unmistakable. 'I know what you must think. I was a good soldier up until a few months ago.' He had to tell her everything 'The group of lads I was in charge of was on night patrol. We travelled in tanks, armoured

138

trucks and jeeps, to ensure that the villages and our base were safe.'

'Where were you stationed?' Tammy asked.

'Afghanistan; I was sent there about three months after my passing out parade.'

'Why didn't you tell me? Why didn't you write to me?' The words came out of her mouth before she could stop them. But she knew why he hadn't written or told her where he had been going. *Weren't you the one who broke up with him?* she thought to herself.

Jason didn't want to talk about that now; he needed to talk to her, to tell her what happened. She had always listened and helped him with his problems. 'We were ambushed.' Jason paused. He needed to do this, needed to relive the nightmare so that she'd understand. 'The whole patrol was caught in it. We'd checked the road for bombs, yet somehow they still managed to blow up our vehicles. I tried to get to my squad mates, but a piece of shrapnel made it impossible. I managed to get to the radio, which thankfully still worked, and called for help.' Tears welled up in his eyes. 'By the time help arrived, I was the only one left alive.' He tried to swallow the lump in his throat; it made it impossible to talk anymore. He glanced down purposefully at his leg; the scar was big enough not to miss and would serve as a constant reminder of the horrors of war.

She shook her head. 'You blame yourself. Can't you see you were injured as well? How could you help them?' Tammy hopped off the wall. 'How could you have stopped those people setting off the bombs?' She thought Jason took too much upon himself at times. 'Jason, you did everything you could and called for help whilst you were in pain.' Tammy wanted to reach out for him, wanted him to hold her, but she was scared that they would kiss again. Her lips still tingled and her skin was on fire.

'Who else is to blame?' Jason kicked

the wall. 'I was in charge. I let them die!'

'No, Jason, you didn't let them die. You did all you could.' She stroked his arm, trying to comfort him, but keeping a little distance between them.

Tears flowed freely down his face. He didn't think it was very manly, but he didn't care anymore. It felt good to finally get things off his chest and release his pent-up emotions. Tammy had always understood him; she'd always been there if he'd needed a sensible solution to a problem. He hadn't seen things the way she had; he'd been injured, the shrapnel embedded in an artery. He could have died himself had he moved any further than to reach for the radio.

'Are you going back?'

He shook his head. 'I don't know. I have to go to a meeting; I'm almost positive they'll discharge me on medical grounds.'

'What are you going to do?'

He saw the confusion on her face.

'I'm going to try and get my job back here. I'd be no good at a desk job; I love being outside too much.'

Tammy smiled. There could be a force ten gale and Jason would still prefer being outside gardening or painting. He'd always been great at D.I.Y, and a few other things that came to mind as well. She tried to push those thoughts to one side. If she didn't they would end up kissing, even if it was very enjoyable. So much for the hard line she had planned to take if they ever saw each other again.

'Why don't we finish our picnic? I'll text mum and see if I can drop Toby off earlier; she won't mind and we can talk some more,' Tammy offered kindly.

'Oh okay, we've been away from the wee man long enough.' He nodded in Toby's direction.

Luckily, Toby had done what he had been asked; he'd found a game to play and was happily digging into the dirt with a stick. It had kept him occupied whilst Tammy and Jason had spoken.

She'd remembered the haunted look in his deep blue eyes when she had first seen him again in the fast food place, and this explained it.

'Mummy, I'm hungry!' A shout was all that was needed to pull them both back to reality. Tammy sat down on the rug and held her son tightly; she wasn't the only one that was harbouring guilt. Handing out the sandwiches, the chatter turned to Toby's love for fire engines. Toby jumped up and ran around the picnic rug, pretending he was going to rescue a cat. The small gesture had been gratefully received, and Jason decided he'd had enough of Toby having all the fun, chasing after him. Slowly the sun began to set; the sky had turned a bright crimson.

'Come on, you two. Let's get you to Grandma's, Toby.' Tammy reluctantly packed away the picnic things. It had been a good day, even if it had been emotional one. Jason had carried his burden for too long; now hopefully the recovery would begin. She didn't want to ask him if he had nightmares about it, or whether he spent his days thinking of all the bad things that had happened. The war was still raging over there; the people didn't want to give up. Many soldiers had died fighting for freedom, and the selfish part in her was glad that Jason hadn't been one of them.

'You'd have liked the passing out parade Tam. All those men in uniform,' Jason said suddenly.

Tammy couldn't help but smile. 'I know. I enjoyed my time there,' she said.

Spinning round on his heels, Jason stared, his mouth open wide. Tammy put her hand over her mouth as she tried to stifle her giggles.

'What do you mean, you enjoyed your time there?' Jason's bewildered look was extremely endearing and sent shivers of pleasure down her spine.

'I was there, Jason.' Tammy caught the look of surprise on Jason's face 'Your mum came around to tell me that you had your passing out parade and

144

asked if I'd like to go. I stayed concealed at the back of the crowd.' She reached out, brushing his cheek with her hand. 'I was so proud of you.'

It had been so hard to watch him go, but Tammy had thought she'd been doing the right thing. Jason had followed his dream, and although now she understood it hadn't turned out the way he had wanted, she hadn't been in his way.

'I wish you'd have come to talk to me,' he said sadly.

'Jason, that wouldn't have been right. I felt like I was intruding as it was, although I must admit you looked pretty hot in your dress uniform.' She ran her tongue over her lip and sent his emotions into overdrive. It was a shame they were in public, he thought. Warmth filled Jason. He decided that, no matter how hard he tried, he just couldn't stay away from Tammy any longer; he needed her. Truth be told, he didn't want to stay away. He'd realised that Tammy was the missing piece of his life. She was the one person who'd kept him grounded when it looked like he'd get into trouble. She'd even got him out of trouble several times with Mr Sherriden, the design teacher, and she'd talked him out of ideas that wouldn't have worked. Jason stopped walking and turned to face Tammy. He pulled her back towards him, leaned towards her slowly, and kissed her, hungrily claiming her mouth.

Maybe the way they had just kissed, and the fact she had gone to his passing out parade, meant she didn't hate him as much as he thought she did? For years Jason had assumed that she had stopped loving him. He had wanted a future with her, but that hadn't happened, and they'd gone their separate ways.

*   *   *

Tammy couldn't think; her mind was in turmoil. She couldn't keep things a secret between them anymore; she'd have to tell Jason. She hoped he'd take it well; her biggest fear was that Jason wouldn't forgive her for the deception. Tammy swallowed hard, trying to get rid of the lump stuck in her throat. She was scared that she would lose everything. It looked like everything she and Toby had ever wanted was within a fingertip's reach, but could be lost in a moment.

She'd have to tell him. If she wanted Jason to be with her again, she needed to let him in on all her secrets, especially the biggest one of them all. She just hoped he'd forgive her for hiding this from him. Could he ever forgive her for the horrible way she had let him go?

6

As they drove to her mother's, Tammy's mind was in torment. She knew she shouldn't have kissed Jason, but the chemistry between them was unmistakeable. She was doing her best to hide her feelings, and so far she thought she'd done a good job. Her lips tingled and the hairs on her arms wouldn't go down.

Finally, she understood what Jason had gone through in the army. How helpless he must have felt, knowing that by moving even an inch further, he would not have survived. She could sympathise with him, but she had no words that would be able to comfort him. All Tammy could do was be there for him.

She thought it ironic that they had both gone through life-changing experiences, but had hidden their feelings from those closest to them.

'Tam, are you ok?' asked Jason, breaking into her thoughts.

Tammy loved the way her old nickname rolled off his tongue. 'I'm fine, Jason; I was just thinking, that's all.'

'You still up for our date?'

'Are you sure you want to go out for dinner with someone like me?'

Jason gripped the steering wheel so tight that his knuckles turned white. 'Tam, stop putting yourself down! I'm sick of hearing you talk like this.' Looking in his rear-view mirror, he saw the look of anguish on her face and wanted to wrap her in his arms. *I will show you just how special you are*, he thought to himself.

'I won't say anything then,' retorted Tammy, hurt by the tone in his voice.

'Come on, darling, let's not fight. I just want the old Tammy back, the one who always laughed at my silly jokes; you hardly ever smile these days, let alone laugh.' Jason was trying to reach her, but every time he thought he was

149

getting close, the barriers were quickly closed around her. He had no idea how to get through to her; trying to have a laugh, albeit at her expense, hadn't worked. She didn't really want to talk about herself, and insisted on trying to keep certain things private. Looking after Toby and helping out at the fire station seemed the only things that made her happy. Mrs Morgan had told him enough for him to understand just how sad and depressed she was.

'How about we go for a takeaway? I noticed an all-you-can-eat buffet restaurant that's opened up in town, if you prefer that.'

'Sure. I've got some menus somewhere; we can have a look at them when we get back to my house once we've dropped Toby off.' Tammy pulled a piece of grass out of her hair. 'You're right; I don't think going out with bits of grass and leaves on us is a very good look.'

Jason chuckled. 'Of course, I wouldn't want to upset Madam, now would I?'

He found the leaf in her hair very endearing. 'I think we tired the little man out. He's fast asleep.'

Jason was jealous of Tammy — of the joy Toby must give her, and of the fact that she had someone who'd always be there for her. He was glad Debbie had seen fit to give guardianship to Tammy should anything happen to her. It must have been providence. Toby had kept Tammy level; he dreaded to think what might have happened to her if she hadn't had someone who needed her.

'Yes, it looks like we have; he always enjoys going to the park. I know we do it a lot, but kids spend more time inside these days watching TV or on computers than playing games out in the fresh air.'

'How old are you, Tam?'

Tammy swiped him on the arm. 'That is cheeky; it's rude to ask a lady her age,' she said, attempting to sound stern and failing miserably. After all, he already knew her age and had no need to ask; she would find a way to get him back.

'I apologise profusely.' The car suddenly filled with the sound of their combined laughter.

Jason pulled up outside Mrs Morgan's, got out of the car, gently lifted the sleeping boy out of his seat, and carried him to the door. It was nice that Tammy's mum had her grandson, allowing her daughter precious 'me' time. Tonight she was his; he had the overwhelming desire to make love to her, to show her how beautiful she still was, yet he wasn't going to push her into something she didn't want. Being able to spend time with her, to show her that he still cared, would be enough; it would have to be. He waited for Tammy to knock on the door.

'Hi Mum,' Tammy said with a warm and tender smile.

'My little treasure's tired; take him to his room, Tammy, and put him in bed.' Jason saw the wry smile on Mrs

Morgan's face. 'Jason, it was very nice of you to drop Toby off.'

'It was my pleasure; we've just come from the park.' Well it was the truth; he wasn't going to lie. 'Tammy and I are going out for dinner.'

'Well, I hope you kids have a good time.'

Just as they were talking, the lady in question appeared. 'Did I hear my name mentioned?'

'I was just telling your mum we're going out for dinner,' Jason replied.

'Well, were just going out for a catch-up.' Tammy tried her best to emphasise 'catch-up'. Who was she was trying to convince, herself or her mother?

'Well, you kids have fun.' With a smile, her mother disappeared behind the front door.

They arrived at Tammy's house fairly quickly; she had been extremely quiet on the way home, and Jason didn't really want to intrude on her private thoughts. 'I'm just going to run up and get changed,' she said.

Jason detected a hint of hesitancy in her voice; he wanted Tammy to have a good time. He wandered around her living room, looking at all the pictures of Toby. There must have been at least twenty of them lining the walls, and several larger ones on top of the fireplace. The fire engine he had won at the auction lay on the floor, so he carefully picked it up and moved it so that no one would step on it.

The room was simply decorated. *It looks like Tammy has a thing for minimalist decor, which is more than can be said for her dress sense,* he thought to himself. Sitting on the large black leather sofa, he picked up the paper and started to peruse its pages. He assumed she'd take a long time dressing, since she was female, but no sooner had she gone up did she flounce back into the room fully changed.

Great, another ugly cardigan, he thought. *Doesn't she wear anything else?* 'You don't need to wear that,' he said sounding harsher than he intended. 'It isn't cold and you don't have to hide anything from me.' Jason regretted the words as soon as he'd uttered them. He couldn't take them back and he felt it was about time Tammy faced her problem, rather than try to run away from it all the time the way he had.

'What . . . What do you mean?' she stuttered.

'I know about the fire, Tam.' He moved slowly towards her, but stopped just before he reached her. 'I know why you hide yourself by wearing those ugly things.' He wanted to give her chance to turn away from him, and leave the room if she must.

Tammy's voice cracked. 'I know what this is; to you it's a sympathy date!' she exclaimed through thin lips. 'The only reason you want to take me out is so everyone can laugh at poor old Tammy.'

Jason was surprised at the venom in her voice, and that she could think so lowly of him. Did she honestly believe all he wanted to do was make fun of her? 'No, Tam; just listen to yourself. I asked you out because I wanted to be with you. I don't care about anything else.' Jason had decided it was time to wear his heart on his sleeve. When he thought about it, it did sound rather cliche, but he didn't care. There wasn't another way to put it: he wanted to spend the rest of his life with Tammy. Unfortunately, treading carefully wasn't one of his virtues.

'I don't want to go out.' She pointed to the door. 'Jason, just leave. I am not someone who can amuse you. And I don't need your sympathy.' Tears flowed freely down her face. She wrapped her arms around her body, trying to protect herself from his onslaught.

'Come on, Tammy; don't cry. Let's just go have some fun. Wear the stupid thing if it's so important.' Jason could have kicked himself for saying something so cruel. Tact wasn't always his strong point. 'Tam, I want to show you something.' Jason said quietly. 'That came out a bit wrong.'

'What did you want to show me?' Tammy replied hesitantly.

'Now, don't get any ideas,' Jason replied as he slowly removed his jeans, revealing the large unsightly shrapnel scar on the inside of his leg. The skin grafts had worked well, but there was still a lot of pitting and discoloration to his leg.

Tammy's hands flew to her mouth. 'Jason, I . . . I . . . '

There were no words; nothing that she could say which would soothe him. She had been so wrapped up in her own injury, her own inner demons, that she hadn't thought that someone else could possibly be suffering from the same fate.

'Are you shocked, Tammy?'

'Your leg,' Tammy gasped. 'Jason.' She couldn't believe that he had been hurt so badly, and yet could still smile and laugh about his injury.

'Tam, I still wear shorts with this,' Jason added proudly. 'My battle scar and a limp to match.'

'You seem proud of it, but how can you appear so nonchalant?' asked Tammy.

'Because I survived, Tammy. I'm here! Standing in your living room! A lot of the lads haven't been as lucky as me. They've lost their lives and limbs, and I've managed to get out with only a scar on my leg and bad dreams.' He gave her a wry smile. 'Compared to them I've been lucky, and you have to see that yourself.'

Jason walked slowly towards her, and leaning over her, he whispered in her ear, 'But you're beautiful. Don't hide yourself.' His body ached for her; he wanted to make love to her to show her that she was as desirable to him now as she'd ever been.

'Look, if all you wanted to do was make fun of me, you could have done it that day in the fast food restaurant.' Her voice had become high-pitched through crying.

'Tam, I'd never make fun of you.' Jason thought for a moment. Okay, he'd played practical jokes on her and hidden green slime in her shoes, but this was serious. What did she take him for?

'So, why are you here? What do you really want?' Tammy's voice rose.

'I told you, Tammy. I am on leave, perhaps for good, and I wanted to see you, to spend time with you.'

Tammy just looked at him, bewildered. 'Why? What's so special about me?'

'Oh Tammy, won't you ever see yourself clearly?' Jason was exasperated. He reached up slowly and started to unbutton the cardigan. He felt Tammy flinch, but she didn't move away from him. With great care, he pushed the piece of clothing over her shoulders and pulled out her arms. She tried wrapping her arms around herself to hide the hideous red scars she bore on her arm. Jason pulled her hands down.

'Don't, Tam. Come to the mirror,' he whispered tenderly, walking her over to it. He stood behind her. Each time she

159

brought her hands and put them around her body, he tenderly removed them. She tried to cover up the scars, but he wanted her to see clearly, perhaps for the first time in a long time. 'See how beautiful you are, Tam?' He kissed her ear and moved slowly down to her neck, placing small delicate kisses along her shoulder and the top of her arm.

'I'm not; I'm hideous.' Tammy shook Jason off her; he needed to know the truth. 'Do you know it was my fault?' She waited for his answer, waited for the accusations to start, but he stayed quiet, staring intently at her. 'I'm to blame! Debbie is dead because of me.'

'How could it be your fault? It was an accident.'

'We had gone out to a friend's birthday party.' Her eyes dropped to the floor. She couldn't face him, to see the look of disappointment in his eyes. 'When we came back we were both hungry, but we couldn't afford a take-away, so whilst Debbie went upstairs to change, I made homemade chips and put the chip pan on.' Sobs wracked her body as she finally gave a voice to all the sorrow she had held deep inside her heart. 'I . . . ' She choked on the words. 'I fell asleep. When I woke up, the house was well alight. I tried to get out, but I couldn't. I couldn't even reach Debbie.'

'Shush, baby. It was an accident. Please believe me; it wasn't your fault.' Jason put his arms around her and held her till her sobs finally abated. Placing a row of kisses down the nape of her neck, Jason could feel her squirm underneath him. He continued to kiss her until he turned her around so that she was facing him. She tried to cover herself again, but he moved her hands and placed them round his waist.

'Why don't we stay here and eat in?' He kissed her forehead; he didn't want to share her with anyone else. He needed Tammy to see how desirable she was, so she'd regain the confidence she'd lost. He leaned down and roughly claimed her mouth, his need taking over every rational sense. His hands wandered slowly and exquisitely painfully over her back, sending shivers along her spine. A white heat burned in her belly as he continued his delicious onslaught. She couldn't think straight; for a time she forgot where she was. The only thing Tammy knew was that she never wanted this to end.

'Okay,' she murmured between his kisses. 'What? I was just beginning to enjoy that.'

He detected the disappointment in her voice, but he tried to reassure her. 'There will be plenty more of that later. I don't know about you, but I could really use some food.'

For the first time that night, Tammy smiled. Jason was always thinking about his stomach; she wondered if it was just a guy thing or a Jason thing.

The room plunged into silence whilst Tammy tried to process what Jason was saying. Finally, she understood what he'd been trying to tell her. It didn't matter about her arm or the scar on her chest. She didn't need to hide from anyone. Yes, she'd probably be stared at for a while by strangers, but if she let them know it didn't bother her, then eventually they would stop. Even if she had to let Jason go back to the front line, she could, knowing that he'd come back even for a short time and helped her.

His kisses showed her that he still cared about her. Even after all the aggravation she'd just given him, he still wanted to spend time with her.

'Are you going to place the order for the takeaway?' She went to pick the cardigan on the floor. Jason reached over and tried to stop her.

'Don't worry Jason, I am not going to put it on. I just don't like leaving clothes on the floor.'

'I'm sorry; I didn't mean to upset you.'

Flinging her arms around him, she squeezed his neck tightly and kissed him gently on his cheek. 'I'm not upset. For the first time in a long time I feel I can be me.' She found the confused look on his face endearing. 'I may put some cover-up on it just so it doesn't appear so red, but I believe this,' said Tammy holding up the cardigan, 'can be consigned to the wardrobe until it is cold enough to actually wear it.' Tammy felt free for the first time in a long time, as though she was a bird on its wing.

Don't think just because you aren't going to cover up, that you'll get a man to love you. The insidious voice in her head gave her a warning, but Tammy chose to ignore it; she would no longer be a slave to that voice. Learning to live again would be hard, but it was her choice to do so. She had no idea what was happening. Before, she would have run away from Jason or any man; but now, she wanted his touch — needed him to want her, and needed his lips on hers. He made her feel alive. She was falling in love with him all over again, and that was something she would have to stop. Falling too hard for him when he re-joined his regiment would be devastating. She couldn't allow her feelings to run away from her. *You have to tell him, you know that don't you?* For once the voice in her head was right; Jason had a right to know.

Jason smiled; he was happy Tammy was finally seeing sense. How long had her life been put on hold because of the fire? Would she have kept it on hold forever? Jason would have known her parents had tried to help her, but they could only do so much if she wasn't willing to help herself.

'Tam, come here.' Tammy shook her head and moved out of reach.

Jason reached out and pulled her back to him, wrapping his arms around her. He pulled her into his warm embrace. They sat for what seemed like hours in silence, enjoying the moment. Tammy felt happy. Perhaps she was wrong, but it seemed as if Jason still felt the same as he had done all those years before. Tomorrow she would tell him, but just for tonight she wanted to enjoy what they had, because tomorrow she knew it would be gone.

Leaning towards her, he teasingly brushed his lips across her cheek, a sly smile on his face, 'That is all you're going to get until you feed me, woman.'

'That is so not fair, Jason.'

'You should know by now I don't play fair,' Jason retorted.

Tammy laughed and waltzed out of the front room, clattering around in the kitchen drawers for a takeaway menu. 'Jason, what do you fancy? Chinese or Indian?'

'You,' he answered flippantly.

'Come on, be serious.' Tammy tried not to laugh. 'Come in the kitchen and look at the menus.'

Jason complied obediently. Taking a menu, he glanced briefly over it. 'How about a banquet meal, with maybe some oysters?'

'I think the way that you're going, you don't need any oysters.' She said, trying desperately to stifle a giggle as she continued to tease Jason. She handed him the phone. 'Come on and make yourself useful whilst I get the plates and things ready.' She didn't drink much, but she always had a bottle of wine in the house just in case her parents ever came round for dinner. She presumed a soldier boy would like a drink; he could always get a taxi home.

A knot formed in her stomach. She was nervous anticipating what would happen between them. It was too easy for her to get lost in the way he looked at her. Having placed everything on her kitchen table, she carried the glasses and wine into the front room. She caught Jason's approving glance as his eyes roamed over her body. She swallowed tightly as he sat down beside her, feeling the heat between them. It was perilous to have feelings like this for him; it was at the back of her mind he would leave soon and she dared not get too close.

'What's wrong, Tam?' Jason asked, concern etched on his face.

'Nothing. I'm all right; I was just thinking,' she said, shrugging her shoulders. She didn't want him prying too much into her thoughts. He had already broken down more barriers in a few short hours than she was prepared for.

The doorbell rang, signalling that their meal had arrived — a welcome interruption to the silence which had descended on them. Jason jumped up. 'I'll get this, Tam,' he said, reaching in his back pocket for his wallet.

Picking up the glasses, Tammy made her way into the kitchen; it was nice to have a man around, even if it was only for a meal. She would be sad when it was all over. She told herself that nothing lasts forever and that even though Jason was showing her the first bit of tenderness she'd experienced for a long time, he wouldn't be staying. She couldn't see that the military would discharge him even if he was suffering from PTSD.

Shaking her head, she realised that she needed to concentrate on what they were doing now, not what would happen in the future. *Carpe diem*. Jason walked in, a cardboard box in his arms. 'I didn't realise that we had ordered so much.'

'Well, to feed a bottomless pit, then yes we needed to order so much.'

After their Chinese, she took out the chocolate cake Mrs Anderson had made for her. It would make for a nice after-dinner dessert.

Jason reclined on the chair. 'I couldn't eat any dessert, Tam. I'm stuffed.'

Tammy was in a teasing mood. Each bite of the cake she tried, she exaggerated how delicious it tasted, offering Jason a tit-bit of hers, and slowly drawing the fork out of her mouth. A few times she wiped the corners of her mouth with a napkin, very slowly. Tammy decided that eye contact was the way to gain Jason's attention. Her gaze fixed on his as she tried the final piece of cake. The song 'Love is All Around' was playing softly on the radio. Taking a forkful of the frosting, she offered it to Jason, who shook his head.

'Come on, Jason,' Tammy whispered. 'You know you want to.' Again, Jason shook his head.

'No,' he stated.

'What do you want, Jason?' Tammy asked.

'You.' Jason's hand snaked around the back of her head and drew her towards him. His lips touched hers and ignited the flames of passion so long banked. Tammy responded as their lips danced to an unheard tune. They were each lost in the moment and in their memories.

She needed to know how he felt. She wasn't going to let one leg-weakening kiss cloud her judgment. He had done too much damage with those lips of his. Was a relationship indeed possible? Would the soldier become hers alone? Or would he still insist that he had to serve his country?

When they both came up for air, each had difficulty in catching their breath.

This had certainly not been on Tammy's agenda for the day. The kiss only cemented her feelings that she was irrevocably in love with Jason. Her mum used to say 'time heals all wounds'. Time hadn't healed any of Tammy's wounds or made her feelings dissipate in any way. She was stuck and she couldn't think. She had come up with all the questions but didn't have any answers to them. Not knowing how far could she trust him — Jason had inadvertently broken her heart once — could she take the chance and allow him to have her heart to keep?

* * *

She had no idea of the time, just that daylight was streaming through the curtains. Jason still had his arms wrapped around her. She smiled, realising that they must have fallen asleep on the settee after having snuggled together. Jason lay snoring softly. Her belly growled with hunger.

She untangled herself from his embrace and wandered into the kitchen to make breakfast. She would let him eat first, then tell him. It was the only thing she could do. It wasn't fair to him to keep lying.

★ ★ ★

After Jason had eaten he got up, but Tammy grabbed his arm. 'Jason, sit down. We need to talk.'

Jason didn't miss the ominous tone in Tammy's voice. He'd other things on his mind, but the way she was looking at him made him think he definitely wouldn't like what he was going to hear. Jason sat on the sofa and waited for the bombs to fall around him.

Instead of taking a seat near him, Tammy moved to the armchair opposite. She needed a little distance from him. 'It's about Toby.'

'What's wrong with him?'

'Nothing, he's fine.' She caught the panic in his voice. 'It's just that I need to talk to you about him.' She gulped for air.

'Go on. All this seems rather strange.' Jason dreaded what was to come.

'You know when I said Toby was Debbie's child?' Tammy waited for his acknowledgement.

'Yes.'

'He isn't Debbie's, Jason. Toby is my son.' She let the words rush from her mouth. If she said it quickly, he might not be able to process what she was telling him.

'What! You told me . . . '

She sensed his confusion and anger. 'I know, I know.' Tammy stood up and went to sit beside him. 'There's more. Toby has never known the name of his father.'

'You didn't waste any time getting someone else then, did you?' Tammy saw the look of utter disgust on his face. 'Is that why you split up with me? Because you wanted someone else?'

'Jason, no. I've never been with anyone else,' she said. At least that was the truth.

'So, what is it you're trying to say?'

'Toby is your son, Jason.' Tammy's shoulders shuddered as she tried to hold back the tears.

'No! That's impossible. He isn't my son.' He stood up and paced around the front room. 'I can't be a father.' He held his hands tightly down by his sides. 'No, you must have cheated on me.'

'Jason, please believe me,' Tammy implored.

'No! How can I believe you when you've already lied to me about who the mother was?' Jason's voice became shrill as his anger rose.

'I'm telling you the truth.' Tammy got up and walked towards him, placing her hand gently on his arm.

'Don't touch me!' he cried as he shrugged her hand off him. 'Why are you saying these things? If you didn't want to see me, you could have said so. Instead, you invent all these lies just to get rid of me.' He headed to the living room door; he'd heard enough. 'Toby isn't mine, and you've got your wish now, haven't you? I hope you're happy.' With that, he walked out, slamming the front door behind him.

Tammy stood motionless in the living room, her tears flowing freely. Why had he denied that Toby was his? Didn't he know her better than that? She'd loved him with every fibre of her being. Why did he think that she would treat him so badly? She had only done it for him and not for any other reason. Tammy slumped in the armchair. Bringing her knees to her chest and holding on tight, she continued to chastise herself.

7

Jason stared back at Tammy's house. He was absolutely gobsmacked that she had told him so many lies. He thought they knew one another better than that, but obviously that wasn't the case. Well, she'd certainly rid herself of him now! He wanted to put as much distance between them as possible. He wanted to get on a bike and ride into the sunset the way they always did in the movies.

That was an idea; he'd go out and buy himself a motorbike, see how she'd like that! He remembered all the things Tammy hated. He'd love to see her face; a motorbike would really make her blood boil. She'd always said they were dangerous. Well he supposed they were, but only if he came off it. Who else would care, except perhaps his family? He'd lost Tammy and all the fun he'd intended to have with Toby. All his grand plans had gone out of the window.

Jason got in his car. He had no idea where he was going; he drove around and headed out into the country. The audacity of Tammy's revelations were what had upset him the most. He couldn't be a dad; he wasn't capable of looking after himself, let alone a small child. Well the boy wasn't that young, but how could Jason be there? What would he do if Toby was sick? Or what if he needed someone to watch his school plays and go to parents' evenings? Jason kept telling himself that he wouldn't be any good — not to Tammy or Toby.

No, Jason knew he was better off without a woman complicating his life. He'd promised himself when he'd come home that there wouldn't be anyone; he wouldn't let anyone get close to him. Jason thought he'd become emotionally attached to Tammy because of their past, but it would pass quickly enough — at least, he hoped it would.

He put his foot down, increasing his speed along the country roads. His music blared from the car stereo. It usually helped him relax, but he was still as tense as ever. The sky had turned black, as the stars shone in the night sky. He knew that the dreaded meeting at the military base was in the morning, but the lack of sleep wouldn't bother him. He wished he could close his eyes for one more night of peaceful, uninterrupted sleep, but that wouldn't happen. That did happen last night with Tammy — they both had fallen asleep on the sofa, and she had kept the horrific dreams away. He was grateful to her for that. He'd do anything to avoid having to cope with the memories. Jason watched all of the boring night-time programmes on the television, or played video games late into the night. He'd become addicted to caffeine and drank copious amount of coffee.

No! This new Tammy had dropped a bombshell, and he knew that there was no way he could be Toby's father. He wasn't fit to do anything, except cause his parents heartache, because of how he was behaving. Sadly, he drove home, letting the anger from Tammy's lies boil up inside him. First there'd been the rubbish that Toby was Debbie's child, and now to top it all off, she was trying to blame it on him. Him? A father? It was laughable. Just because Toby's real dad had done a runner, what was that to him?

Jason banged his hand on the steering wheel. Driving back into town, he heard the large church in the centre of town chime twelve midnight. He needed to get home; he had to set off early in the morning. He hadn't been prepared for all the curveballs life had decided to throw at him today. By this time tomorrow, he'd know if he was still in the army, or if he'd just be your average person on the street. His life was already a mess, and with Tammy's confession, it had taken on a whole new meaning. No! He wasn't Toby's father, and he didn't want to be. Toby was happier knowing that Debbie was his mum, even if she wasn't here to look after him herself.

Jason sat and pondered on things. Toby had never said his mum had died. In fact, he never mentioned Debbie at all. He wondered if this was what Mrs Morgan meant. Maybe she had thought he was the father, but didn't want to say anything to him. Perhaps she thought that it was Tammy's job to come clean. What were his parents going to say? But there was absolutely no point in upsetting them with a pack of lies. Jason headed home; he needed a few strong coffees to see him through the night.

★   ★   ★

Jason left the house early that morning, before his parents had got up. Jumping in his car, he put his favourite Dance 95 CD on; it helped him to relax. He had to admit that, although it was old, he preferred songs where you could actually hear what they were saying. Being in the car meant he could crank up the volume as loud as he wanted it without resorting to headphones. His parents had mentioned to him, more often than not, that the music was too loud. As soon as he could, he'd be moving out. No matter how much he loved them, their constant vigilance over his health and state of mind was wearing on what little sanity he had left.

He regretted driving his poor mother to distraction, as every day he refused to go to bed, but last night had been the turning point — or at least he hoped it would be. He couldn't remember anything at all, except waking up this morning feeling refreshed for the first time in months. No bad dreams, no echoes of the past. He felt strange that he could now see a future, and with any luck that future wouldn't include Tammy and Toby. He didn't want them anywhere near him.

He thought about the last night they'd spent together all those years ago, and his whole body tingled in anticipation of a repeat performance. He'd been lucky; there would be no way back for them. Tammy had made that clear when she'd spun her web of lies. Women! They always let you down. Jason turned to look at himself in the mirror. He needed to calm down and stop thinking about it. There was one thing he still wanted to know: how cosy was she with all those firemen? His anger threatened to boil over and consume the happy thoughts he had been having just minutes earlier. Jason still couldn't put his finger on what was really going on, but he was determined to discover their secret.

He stopped at the services on the way down to Colchester for light refreshments. There was no way he was going to stay any longer than was absolutely necessary. He wanted get back home to the people he loved; he was saddened that most of his friends had left town. Those who'd stayed had found new friends. He hadn't bothered to stay in contact with anyone from the past, and his only social life since he'd been back consisted of a day at the park, and a day and a night at a firemen's fundraiser. Jason stifled his laughter; he definitely was the life and soul of the party.

After a couple of hours, he pulled into the winding drive of the army barracks. His heart pounded hard against his ribcage, not because he was scared, but because he desperately wanted out of the army. He'd had enough; the life he'd once led was gone, and all he had to show for it was the uniform, and no one to call his own — no girl to come home to and put his arms around, no kids to read bedtime stories to and tuck in at night.

Reaching the top of the small hill, Jason found his way blocked by barriers and two burly armed guards in full military attire who stood in his way.

'Papers, please,' they asked in unison.

Jason took his military card out of his wallet, and along with his driving license, he handed them to the guards.

'Who are you here to see?'

'General Hulme and the field doctor.' His answer was as brief and offhand as theirs; he knew that they were only doing their job, but as his gran always used to say, 'Manners cost nothing.'

They went into the guard post to make a phone call. Jason didn't hear what they were saying, but he knew that they were only checking that everything was on the up and up. The guard returned and handed Jason his papers, and he tossed them onto the passenger seat; he wanted this over as soon as possible. The gates opened, allowing him passage onto the base. Security had definitely been tightened, with two armed guards posted now instead of one.

He drove slowly around the sleeping quarters and mess hall until he reached the doctors' offices. The army insisted on a full medical check-up before he saw the general. The waiting room looked like any other one: there were hard plastic chairs lined up against one wall, whilst on the other were diagrams of skeletons and internal organs. Jason wondered if that was for the hypochondriacs amongst them, so they could feign an illness.

The secretary was an older woman with salt-and-pepper hair and a dour demeanour. The doctors he'd seen tended to select their secretaries based on their work efficiency and not their appearance. It was probably a good thing; it was a shame that not everyone was efficient and punctual. Jason hated being late for anything and always arrived early for appointments, which usually meant he'd wait for people to get round to him. Why was it that whenever you were early, the people you wanted to see were always running late? He supposed it was one of the great mysteries of the universe.

The doctor, dressed in a white coat, his stethoscope hung loosely around his neck, came into the room.

'Corporal Rivera, come with me, please.'

Jason followed him into his office; his limp was more pronounced than usual, but he put it down to the long drive and sitting in the same position for hours. Even his brief stop hadn't been long enough to avoid the tingling sensation that ran up and down his leg.

'Would you mind removing your trousers and then hopping up here on the bed?'

Jason complied. The doctor examined his wound and made Jason press his foot against him to see how strong he was, and whether or not he had lost any feeling in his leg.

'How's that?'

Jason replied, 'It still hurts when I put too much pressure on it, but otherwise, I manage.'

'Good, good.' The doctor made Jason do numerous physical and mental tests before writing several notes in his file. He called his secretary in, handed her Jason's medical file, and ordered her to have it delivered forthwith to the general.

Jason wondered why he hadn't just asked him to take it with him, but then again this was the army, and it was probably against protocol.

He left his car outside the doctors' offices, preferring to walk around the area until he reached the general's office. It might help get rid of this bloody cramp, he thought. Several squads of soldiers, probably new recruits, passed him as they marched around the base. Jason silently wished them good luck; they'd need it if they were sent over there. He walked confidently into the office.

'I have an appointment to see General Hulme,' Jason stated to the secretary.

'Name?' she asked in a most business-like manner.

'Corporal Rivera.'

'Just one moment, please.'

With quick efficiency, the secretary rang through, and in a matter of moments he stood to attention before the general, waiting for the order to be seated — or would he be expected to stand during the interview? It wasn't easy to get compassionate leave, let alone a medical discharge. The army didn't like losing soldiers, and here he was wishing they would just let him go back to Civvy Street, so he could forget the past and try to make a new life for himself.

'At ease, soldier.' The general stood, picked up an ornate walking stick, and tucked it under his arm. 'Sit down, Corporal, please.' He used his stick to point to the chair.

'Thank you, sir.'

'I've been going through your medical records,' he said, his voice etched with authority.

'Yes, sir,' Jason replied, but what he really wanted to say was, 'Oh come on, let's get this over with. Cut out the red tape and discharge me.' Jason thought better of pushing the general; it wasn't a good idea. He'd find himself in the guardhouse quicker than he could make a pot of coffee.

'I see you suffered the loss of your

patrol over there.'

'Yes, sir; my patrol was ambushed, and I was the only survivor.' Jason was impatient to be on his way; he'd promised his mum he wouldn't be long, but by the looks of this general, the man would be tearing up his discharge papers and ordering him back to the front lines.

'I see from the doctor's notes that you took a piece of shrapnel in a main artery.'

Jason saw him stare pointedly at him. What did he think he had done? Made it all up?

'Yes sir, I managed to reach the radio and call for help, but unfortunately I couldn't move any further,' he replied. *Though I wish I had*, he thought to himself. *Maybe a few of them would be here if I'd done more.*

The general flicked through the report, humming and arrhing in certain places. 'I understand you also suffer from PTSD, post-traumatic stress disorder? That's what the doctor is saying in any case.'

Jason merely nodded; the report sat right in front of him. Did he need to make any more obvious comments?

'I do hate to lose good men, but I can see from all the reports that you are not fit to carry on.' The general tutted and looked stricken. 'I'd normally offer you a place working in the barracks, but I don't think that would be suitable for you. In an emergency, you could still be called to the front at a moment's notice.'

Jason shook his head.

'I see here that you even hated doing stock checks, so pushing papers around wouldn't be your thing.'

For several minutes, they sat in silence. Jason wanted to tell him to be quick and make a decision, but thought better of it.

'You will, of course, be honourably discharged from the army and have any rights and privileges that go with it applied to you.' The general handed him a stack of papers. Jason was free at least of the army; the memories would take much longer to dissipate.

Jason merely nodded. He had the answer he wanted; he was out. Now, with any luck, he could drive back and be home in time for tea.

'How about joining me for a drink in the mess hall? You've served your country well, Corporal, and I'm sorry to let you go, but needs must.' The general didn't wait for an answer before continuing. 'The least I can do is to see you off with a good drink; I'll pay.'

Jason was gobsmacked and bewildered as he followed the general out of his office, his discharge papers in hand. He smiled inwardly to himself. Now, if only he could get his job back up at the hall, or find work painting — that seemed like a nice one-man job with no one else to look after. He knew his family would be happy; he'd be staying in River Springs permanently, and out of danger.

The general stood waiting patiently at the entrance to the mess hall. Jason found it all very strange; to the best of his knowledge, never before had the general bought an enlisted man a drink. Usually that privilege was for the officers, and even then they usually bought him drinks. A general even going into the normal mess hall was a no-no as well, but Jason definitely wasn't going to complain if he didn't have to pay for the drinks.

As they stood by the bar, several other soldiers stared at them; Jason saw the dark clouds on their faces. He couldn't blame them; it did look as if he was getting preferential treatment from the general — even he thought that. How many people in the barracks had the general bought drinks for? Since he was no longer a soldier, he couldn't care less; let them think what they wanted. After they downed the shot of whiskey, the general ordered another round.

'General, can I stay on the base tonight? That second whiskey is going to put me over the limit.'

'Of course. Do you need to let

anyone know that you're staying?'

'Err, yes; I told them at home I would only be a few hours. Could you just excuse me for a moment, sir?'

Jason wandered to a quiet corner of the bar, took out his phone, and called home. When he'd finished his call, he re-joined the General, finding another whiskey had been ordered for him. Jason knew that since he was no longer part of the army, he wasn't really supposed to stay on the base; luckily for him, the general had used his discretion and had given permission. He'd never drink and drive. If it had been necessary, he'd have slept in his car.

'Rivera, why don't you join me in the officers' mess for a spot of dinner?'

Jason stared at the general. Him? In the officers' mess? Maybe he should have tried to leave the army sooner. They usually had the best food in there — at least three courses. He was starting to think it hadn't been such a bad idea to have that whisky after all.

The mess hall had a shop in one

corner where they could buy all their shampoo and boot polish, as well as almost anything else they'd need. Jason had loved receiving care packages from home. His mum had packed them full of goodies; even when he was stationed abroad, they still got through on supply carriers. It had often made him homesick to receive the letters from his mum and dad, filled with tales of parties and where they were going for a weekend stay, whilst he was stuck in a hot desert, without any home comforts! Jason felt sorry for the new recruits. They didn't know how hard it would be away from their families, but he commended them for having the commitment to fight for their country.

'Follow me, Corporal,' the general shouted as though he was out in the yard doing a drill.

'Yes, sir.'

Jason was hungry, and although it was nice to be on the base, he couldn't wait to be off it again. He would never have to return to war, to the base, or do anything he didn't want to do. From now on, he would do exactly as he pleased.

The three-course dinner was everything Jason could wish for, and more. It had been washed down by several more whiskies, as they drank late into the night. Inebriated, Jason staggered to the sleeping quarters. The beds were basic and not exactly comfortable, but Jason knew he had to lie down quickly, before he fell down. As soon as he hit the bunk, his eyes closed and he fell into a deep, drunken slumber.

When he woke the next morning, Jason couldn't remember anything. He knew that was the second full night's sleep he'd had in months; there had been no dreams, no nightmares. His head ached acutely from all the drinking he'd done, but he couldn't blame it entirely on himself. As soon as he got back, he'd buy himself a bike, and then he could feel the wind rush past him as he sped along the road. He'd often heard that bikers made better drivers anyway, since they needed to be more aware of their surroundings. Well, that was what he'd tell his mother to calm her down when she saw the heap of steel.

8

Tammy hadn't moved since Jason had left. The hours ticked by and day had slowly turned into night. She was still in the exact position that she'd taken after Jason had walked out on her. Her face was stained and her eyes were swollen from the tears she had shed. Why had she hidden the truth from him? It had felt like the right thing to do at the time; she'd let Jason get on with his life, whilst she moved aside.

Tammy stood up and looked at herself in the mirror. 'You've made such a mess of everything. Why did you do it?' she asked her reflection. A wry smile crossed her face; a reflection wasn't going to answer, was it? The voice in her head had been surprisingly quiet, its stark warnings a mere echo of what they had been. She didn't want to hear it again. Jason didn't love her, but maybe someone else could. Who was she trying to kid? There would be no one else for her, and he'd left her for the second time.

A knock on the door brought her swiftly out of her reverie. She walked as slowly as possible towards it, hoping whoever it was would go away. Her first thought was to ignore it, and pretend she wasn't at home.

'I know you're there, Tammy. Open the door!' her mum shouted.

Please, no — anything but a parental lecture, she prayed silently to herself. She turned the lock and opened the door as wide as it would go.

'Hi, mum.'

'Don't you 'hi mum' me! What on earth were you thinking, telling stories to Jason? That was cruel; we've known all along that Toby was his, and when he finds out that you do have a child, what is the first thing you do? You let him think he was Debbie's. Do you realise how hurt her parents would be if they found out about this?' Her mother finally took a breath. 'Come on and sit down whilst I make you a drink. You look like you haven't slept and your hair is a mess.'

That's true, Tammy thought. Her hair *was* a tangled mess, and she still had on her clothes from yesterday. Why had she lied to him? He hadn't deserved that.

'Mum, Jason's made it perfectly clear that he wants nothing more to do with me. Okay, I was wrong to say that Toby was Debbie's, but how was I to know he was going to stay? I don't think that even he is certain that the military would discharge him.' Her shoulders slumped. 'I won't come between him and his career; I didn't then and I am certainly not going to now.'

Mrs Morgan banged the cupboard doors as she made a drink. 'What did you expect? That he would welcome the news that Toby is yours and not Debbie's? How did you expect him to take the news that he had a child when you'd already told him that Toby belonged to someone else?'

'Mum, he had to join the army; why can't you see that? Why is this all my fault?' Even if it were her fault, Tammy didn't want to admit it.

'Look, Tammy, you have to sort it out. What are you going to do when Jason wants to come and see Toby?'

'Jason didn't believe me; he stormed out of here so quickly, I think his feet never touched the ground. If he changes his mind and wants to see his son, I'll drop Toby off at your house, and Jason can pick him up from there.'

Her mother sighed heavily. 'No, you're not doing that. You have a problem, and you need to face it. You're not going to run away from it this time.'

Tammy's nerves were in shreds; her body ached for Jason's touch, but she would have to live without him. At least Toby might get the daddy he wanted, even if she couldn't have Jason.

'Darling, he's back in River Springs and he intends to stay. I had a long conversation with his parents yesterday.

You need to do the right thing; I can't help you with this one. Whatever it is between you has to be sorted out by you both.'

Tammy knew her mother was right, but she had no idea how to fix the mess she'd made. With her cousin gone and Jason no longer in the army, she didn't have anything left. Her mother and possibly her father were on Jason's side. Toby absolutely doted on him, at least for the short while he had been around. She hadn't had the heart to tell him that he had a daddy. Was it possible for a four-year-old to hate you?

'What am I going to do, Mum?' Her head fell in her hands as sobs wracked her body. She needed Jason; she loved him, and now everything was hopeless.

Her mother put her arm around her shoulders and brought her close. 'It will work out Tammy, you'll see. I need to go and get back to your dad; you know he's unwell and I can't leave him for long. Just think about what I said. Toby can stay with me again tonight.'

Tammy kissed her mother good-bye and wandered slowly upstairs. Grabbing the photo albums out of the wardrobe, she threw herself on the bed. She hadn't been brave enough to look at all the pictures before now. She separated the ones she'd done for Jason, placing them in a pile on her dressing table, and then she sat down and opened the bright pink cover. She went through all the photos of her and Debbie, from their double christening to their first high school pictures. Tammy laughed out loud when she looked at herself. They had seemed so carefree, the world was their stage; hadn't Shakespeare said something like that?

Debbie may not have been a physical presence in her life anymore, but she was there in her head and her heart. The fire really hadn't been her fault; it had just been a tragic accident. Jason had made her see that. Terrible things happened every day to others; it just so happened that on that particular day, it was their turn for something bad. Her aunt and uncle, although distraught over the loss of their daughter, had never blamed her, yet she had stayed away through fear and guilt.

Jumping off the bed, Tammy went to grab a cardigan from the wardrobe, but then thought better of it. *This is who I am now*, she thought to herself. It was time she sorted out the fragments of her family and try to pull it all back together. Had it been left too late to mend the threads? Tammy had needed her family a lot over the years, and she'd turned her back on Debbie's parents.

Grabbing her car keys, she dashed out of the front door. In no time at all, she was at her Uncle Mickey's house. Tammy tried to think of what she was going to say, of how she was going to make things right. She had a lot of questions, but no answers to any of them. She hesitated a moment to give herself time to build up some courage. Tammy had left them alone when they had needed her. It had taken the argument with Jason to make her realise she'd been too wrapped up in her own grief to bother about somebody else. Tammy knew she'd been selfish and utterly irresponsible about everything in her life.

Did her aunt and uncle think she didn't care about them or what had happened? Whatever they thought, she was about to find out. Tammy walked slowly to the front door and knocked hard on the lion door-knocker. She twirled her car keys around in her hand, in nervous anticipation agitatedly moving from foot to foot. The door opened slowly. Tammy's stomach fluttered; it was the moment of truth.

'Tammy!' her aunt cried before flinging her arms around her niece.

Tammy was surprised at the reception and hesitantly asked, 'Can I come in, Aunt Mary?'

'Don't be silly, there's no need to ask. We've missed you so much, Tammy.'

Tammy was overwhelmed by the

welcome she received and tears slowly rolled down her face as she looked at the aunt who had been almost like a second mother to her.

'Don't cry, else you will get me going,' said Mary, who'd stood aside to let her prodigal niece past.

Tammy entered the house; walking through the hallway, she could see that her aunt and uncle still had their old-fashioned wallpaper and flowery carpet, a throwback to the seventies. *Not much changes, does it?* she thought.

'Come and sit down, darling. I'll find Uncle Mickey; I'm sure he's going to be as pleased to see you as I am.'

Her aunt left her alone, but she couldn't sit down; instead, she paced up and down the living room, looking at all the photos of Debbie as she'd grown up. Tammy jumped when the door to the living room crashed against the wall; Uncle Mickey strode into the room and embraced her in his strong arms.

'Hi, Uncle Mickey.'

'My dear girl, you have some explaining to do.'

He sounded angry; maybe she shouldn't have come. She'd continue to stay away from them; after all, she'd done enough damage to this side of the family.

'I didn't mean to hurt Deb; it was an accident. We fell asleep. If I could bring her back, I would. I'm so sorry; it was my fault. I said I was hungry and needed to have some food.' Tammy finally took a breath. She waited for the shouting, for the accusations she knew were coming her way. The years hadn't made things any easier; the guilt lay heavy on her. Even though Jason had made her see that the scars didn't look that bad, the one thing he couldn't take away was the guilt. It was why she'd come to lay her soul bare to her aunt and uncle. Tammy needed their forgiveness; she'd inadvertently taken away their only child because of stupidity.

'I didn't mean that! Is that why you

have stayed away? Because you thought we blamed you for the fire?' her uncle asked, mortified.

Her aunt interjected, 'Oh, darling, we never thought that. We were only disappointed because you stopped coming round.'

'You don't blame me? I thought you did, I thought . . . ' but she couldn't finish.

Tammy's uncle put his arms around his niece and his wife followed suit.

'Promise us never to be a stranger again.'

'I won't, I promise.'

Tammy felt relieved that her aunt and uncle didn't hold a grudge. She wouldn't stay long; she had to figure out a way to get Jason to forgive her, and that would be even harder to do.

'Come and sit down. I'll put the kettle on,' her aunt said.

Tammy dropped down onto the sofa; she was glad that things seemed to be fine.

Her uncle sat next to her. 'Now, what

have you been doing with yourself?'

'I help out at the fire station, take Toby to nursery, and help Mum and Dad.'

'It looks like you're keeping yourself busy.'

Mickey was pleased his niece had come round; the house had been devoid too long of the laughter that used to fill it. He hoped that she'd bring her son to see them, so that the house would be filled with tiny footsteps, and bring some much-needed joy back to their lives.

'Tell me about Toby,' he urged.

'Toby loves the fire engines and watching cartoons. He's even started playing football now at nursery,' Tammy replied animatedly.

Her uncle let her talk to her heart's content, until his wife interrupted carrying the tea things. 'Here you go, you two.'

'Thanks, Aunt Mary.' Tammy took a small sip of her tea. 'What have you been doing?'

'Nothing much; some days it's a struggle to do even the most menial tasks, but we don't have what your parents have. They get to have Toby and have something to get up for each morning,' her aunt replied sadly, her shoulders slumped.

'When Toby gets to know you, maybe you could look after him sometimes?' Tammy asked hesitantly.

'Oh, that would be wonderful.'

She saw the smiles instantly appear on her aunt and uncle's faces. The simple gesture of the possibility of looking after a child had lightened the mood, and it seemed she'd indeed given them something to look forward to in the future. Time flew as they chatted and caught up with the goings-on in River Springs. Tammy was glad she'd finally come after all this time.

'I best get off. There is something important I need to do.' Tammy reluctantly stood.

'Can't you stay a bit longer?' Mary let out a sigh.

'No, I have really got to sort something out, although I may have left it too long. To be honest, it's with Toby's dad.'

Mary smiled for the first time in a long time. 'Why? What have you done to poor Jason now?'

The heat rose on Tammy's face. 'What, how did you know?'

'Darling, the only people who didn't know that he was the father were Jason himself and possibly his parents. All your family knew; after all, you never went out with anyone else once he had gone. I remember you being in such a state after you split up, and then the fire.' Aunt Mary hugged her.

'Oh!' Tammy couldn't find the words. She thought she'd hidden it pretty well from everyone, but she obviously wasn't as good at hiding things as she'd thought she was.

'I thought you'd hate me after what happened.'

'Oh darling, no! We love you. I have to admit that it broke our hearts to lose

Debbie, but we lost you as well,' her aunt replied sadly.

The guilt Tammy felt weighed heavily on her, but now for an entirely different reason. She'd stayed away for nothing, hidden away from two people who'd needed their whole family around them, and like a coward she'd fled, leaving them to their own sorrow. *Why have I been so selfish and wrapped up in my own problems? Jason was right! I'm the one who's alive whilst my cousin and best friend aren't.*

'Go on, scoot. Will you bring Toby round soon? It would be nice to hear the patter of tiny feet around here again.'

'Of course, Aunt Mary. How about if I bring him one day next week?'

'We'll be here. Your uncle and I don't get out much these days. There isn't much reason.'

'I hope that I can change that. You're welcome to come around to our house anytime you like; how about I cook a Sunday roast? I'll invite Mum and Dad as well.'

With the promise of a family meal given, Tammy said her last goodbye. She breathed a sigh of relief. At least that conversation had gone well, better than she could ever have hoped. She had no need to stay away from them or avoid family gatherings because they were there. Making the first steps to piece together her broken family wouldn't take the guilt away, but maybe they could all heal together.

She missed Jason, missed his daft jokes and cheeky grin. Why on earth had she been so stupid and lied to him? It was one thing to lie to him back then, but she'd had so many chances to set things right, and she hadn't done it. Now, he didn't want anything to do with her. Jason made her feel special; with him, she didn't have to hide her scars or emotions. She could be the person she used to be, play daft tricks on each other, and have someone there when she was lonely and needed a hug.

There was a huge empty space inside her that even Toby couldn't fill. Tammy knew there'd never be anyone else for her. No other man would ever be able to make her feel the way he did. Her heart felt heavy. She'd been so stupid; she'd told lies — not small white lies, but life-changing lies that had hurt the man she'd always loved. Maybe one day he'd forgive her enough to be friends, if for nothing else than their son's sake.

How would she tell Toby he had a daddy? Would he be angry with her as well? All she could do was talk to him and try to explain as best as she could to her four-year-old son. Her heart was in her throat. Tammy had been relieved that her aunt and uncle didn't blame her. Standing outside their home, she gasped for air. How wrong and how stupid of her to believe her family would have turned their backs on her. It had been Tammy herself who'd turned her back on them when they'd needed her the most.

Tammy thought of contacting Jason, but instead she went home. She'd need courage rather than time. She wandered

9

Jason's mobile phone rang. He answered. 'Hello?'

'Hey Jason, it's Stan. I thought if you were at a loose end, maybe we could go have a drink and a game of pool.'

Jason stood and stared at the phone. What was this? Some sneaky way of Stan's to size him up to see if he was suitable for Tammy? It was not like it mattered now, was it? He wanted to laugh, but thought better of it. Stan seemed to care a lot about her, as though she were his own daughter. Tammy still had secrets, and he hated the fact that he didn't know why Stan was so protective of her; but why should it matter? There'd be nothing between them now. He'd tried to help her, and look at what she'd done; she'd even given him a dressing-down when he'd let her know he knew about her scars.

'Sure, I'm free. I'm always free.'

It was true; he was at a loose end now that she wasn't part of his life. Over the past few weeks, he hadn't seen her; he'd been wrapped up with getting his own life in order, and had given up trying to fight his emotions. No matter what, he loved her, but he'd been unable to share his true feelings.

Being around young Toby those few short days had filled the gap in his life that the loss of his friends had created. He'd come to love that little boy deeply. There was nothing he wouldn't give him, especially now that he understood how he'd lost his mother under horrific circumstances. It wrenched his heart each time he'd heard Toby call Tammy 'Mummy'. Jason knew why she'd lied to him but he could never forgive her for that. He smiled at the remembrance of that sweet little boy. Had he himself been like that when he was small?

'Stan, give me half an hour, and I'll

meet you down at the pool hall.' He turned off his phone and finished draining the last dregs of coffee from his cup. He picked up his jacket and keys, and headed out of the front door. *This should be interesting*, he thought. *The Spanish Inquisition might be preferable to this.*

The M.O.D. had served his discharge papers, their doctors corroborating the decision that he'd never be able to go back. The PTSD he suffered would make him a liability to the rest of the squad. He never thought he'd be happy to be out of the army, yet a huge weight of responsibility and guilt had been lifted from his shoulders. Other people could carry that load; what he really needed was an outside job where he'd answer only for himself. He wasn't the sort of person who wanted to be cooped up in an office — not that there was anything wrong with that, but it just didn't suit him.

Stan stood outside the pool hall waiting for him. He was dressed casually in faded jeans and a grey T-shirt, a total contrast to the fireman's uniform he usually wore. Jason called out to him from the other side of the car park. 'Hi, Stan!'

'Are you ready to get your arse kicked?' asked Stan with a laugh.

'We'll see!' Jason shouted over his shoulder. *So, he thinks he can beat me, does he? Well, we'll see about that*, he thought. It was on now, and Jason didn't like to lose at anything.

The pool hall was practically empty, which suited him down to the ground; at least they'd be able to have a chat while they played. Jason wandered over to the bar and ordered two pints, whilst Stan paid for the table and cues.

'Well, you've got me here. When does the inquisition start?'

'Why? What do you mean?' asked Stan, looking confused.

'Well, I thought you wanted to know my intentions towards Tammy; after all, you seem very protective of her.'

'I'm not. I asked you for a game. I

already know you'll be good for Tammy. I haven't seen her that animated in all the years that I've known her.' He leaned across the table and took his shot. The ball sped around the table and stopped just in front of the pocket.

'So, why did you want me to come out?' Jason was still bewildered.

'I asked you out because it's nice to get out once in a while, and I wanted to talk to you about something, not Tammy,' Stan replied as he leaned over the table to take his next shot.

'Shoot, what do you want to ask?' Stan had him worried. Why on earth would a virtual stranger want him to go out for a man-date, and then leave him hanging?

'I hear you're good with engines as well as gardens,' Stan began.

'Yes.' Jason shrugged his shoulders. 'I'm not bad; we had to fix the trucks ourselves in the army. It's pretty hard to find a garage in the middle of a war zone.'

'Well then, how do you fancy earning

a bit of extra money every now and again?'

Jason was interested. 'That would be great for now, and hopefully I'll pick up some work at the hall to keep me busy. What do you have in mind?'

'I can see having little to do would be a problem. One of the engines isn't running smoothly and I wondered if you'd be interested in giving it a once-over,' Stan replied.

'Sure, that won't be a problem. I know Tammy gets a real buzz from helping you. Now you'll have two of us.' Jason shook his hand to seal the deal.

'I believe it's my turn to buy the drinks.'

★　★　★

Stan reclined in the chair, feeling smug. It felt good to help people. Now, if only he could get Jason to consider becoming a part-time fireman.

The fire service always needed good strong men with big hearts. He

220

wondered how Jason would react to losing someone in a fire. He decided he'd best wait before he brought up that particular idea. Fire-fighting definitely wasn't one of the easiest jobs in the world, but to him it had to be the most rewarding. You changed people's lives — helped them when they needed it by rescuing their pet cat from a tree, or putting out a small bonfire that had gotten out of control. As Jason wandered back, Stan knew it would push him to his limits, but he had to do something. Both of the love birds were miserable and needed to confess their love for each other. He believed that until Jason let go of the past, there was no way forward for them.

'Jason, how about making our next game a little more interesting?' asked Stan.

'How would we do that?' Jason probed.

'If I win,' said Stan, 'you have to come out on a call and help out; if I lose, you can have my help for a day of gardening.' Stan watched Jason mulling it over, his brow furrowed.

'Okay, it's a deal,' he answered. Jason could never pass up a bet, especially one like this where money wasn't involved. Little daft dares for drinks or a forfeit were fun, but gambling away your wages wasn't. 'You break first, Stan.' Jason kept his fingers crossed that he wouldn't lose; going to a fire didn't appeal to him.

Stan's break potted his first ball; four more went down before Jason could get near the table. Cursing inwardly, he had the overwhelming feeling he'd just been hustled. Stan seemed to be a very good pool player, a lot better than he was himself. Having missed his second shot, he had to move over and watch as Stan cleared the table, whilst half of his balls remained.

'My game I believe, Jason,' crowed Stan.

'You don't have to look so smug about it.' Jason had a sneaky feeling he'd just been had. 'How often do you play pool?' he asked.

'Every day down at the station. We're always having little competitions to see who's best or who will wash up for Mrs Anderson,' Stan replied with a laugh.

Jason clapped his hands slowly; he had to admit he'd definitely been hustled. 'So, when do you want me?'

'How about coming to the station tomorrow? Would that work?'

'I guess so, but I still say you've hustled me. Since that's the case, I want a day of gardening from you.'

'Deal,' Stan said. 'I have to admit that I belong to the pub's pool team.' He laughed heartedly. Jason could see the funny side and laughed alongside him.

'Fancy another game?' Stan asked.

Jason didn't speak; instead he racked up the balls again. He didn't want to admit it, but he was having a great time. He usually was quite happy in his own company or with those he loved; an image of Tammy came to mind. He stood up suddenly. *I still love Tammy!* His heart pounded against his rib cage.

The realisation hit him like a speeding train; Jason didn't realise he was still standing.

'Jason, what's wrong? Are you alright?' Stan's voice was tinged with concern.

'No, not really,' he admitted. In for a penny . . . 'You do know that I'm not seeing Tammy anymore, don't you?' Stan nodded. 'The problem is I just can't stop loving her; I never could stop.' He repeated the words out loud as though somehow it would make the revelation more real.

'Well, good for you, boy. Now, that you've realised that you can't let her go, aren't you better off telling the lady in question rather than sitting here with a middle-aged man playing pool?'

Jason caught Stan's wry grin. It had taken him a while to finally figure it out for himself. 'It's too late for that, Stan. If you only knew what she'd done, you'd understand.' Jason paused whilst he tried to process what Stan had just said. 'Hang on; what do you mean, now

I've finally realised it? How would you know how I feel?'

'Listen kid, I've been around the block enough times to know that even on the first day I met you, you were in love with her, yet something held you back.' Stan chortled with laughter. 'Besides, the look on your face when I told you her date was sitting in the fire engine was pure gold.' Stan chuckled away to himself.

Jason laughed. 'Was I that obvious? So why didn't I know it?' He hadn't wanted to fall in love and let anyone near him — at least that was what he'd convinced himself when he'd first come back. Now, he was irrevocably in love with Tammy; it was a shame that he'd never told her how much he loved her, how much he'd always loved her. No matter where he'd been, thoughts of Tammy had never been far away. She'd been permanently transfixed into his heart and mind, but being in the army hadn't exactly been conducive to having a girlfriend. No one had ever matched his ideal anyway; even when he'd dated, Jason had found himself comparing them to Tammy.

Telling someone that you loved them was never easy. He'd thought she loved him, but he'd never been sure. There were barriers still up around her like an impenetrable wall. He wondered if Tammy had thought he'd leave again; it would explain why she'd been so cautious, but it wouldn't explain everything. *Oh, what does it matter now? She isn't the person I thought she was. Tammy is just like all the others.*

Jason couldn't overcome his anger at her betrayal; whatever he'd done, Jason didn't think he deserved to be blamed because she'd a child with someone else who couldn't be bothered to be a dad.

Jason shook himself out of his reverie and turned to Stan. 'Do, you want one more game before we call it a night?'

'No. It's not a fair match anyway; I'll only beat you again.' He laughed loudly. 'How about one more drink, and you can tell me what Tammy's done to cause your face to look like thunder every time her name is mentioned. Then we'd best hit the road; you have an early start in the morning.'

'So you're going to hold me to that, are you?' Jason asked as he casually leaned against the pool table.

'Oh yes; a bet is a bet, and you lost.' Stan caught the look of horror on Jason's face. Although he believed himself to be a man of his word, he seemed scared. No — terrified! What did he think they were going to do to him? There was no way Jason would be able to go out on a real call.

'Don't worry, hopefully it won't be anything bad. Perhaps a cat stuck in a tree or an office fire alarm set off accidentally.'

Jason held his breath. He hoped and prayed that there wouldn't be a serious fire, but secretly he was interested in what Stan and the boys did. He'd had enough talking about Tammy; she was out of bounds — now, if he could only just get her out of his head.

'So what happens if someone starts a fire deliberately?'

Stan shrugged his shoulders. 'The fire investigation officers are usually called in to ascertain the cause of the fire, and then criminal proceedings take place. If they catch whoever committed the crime, they prosecute.'

Mm, interesting career choice, Jason thought. Unfortunately, it probably involved a lot of paperwork, and that wasn't his thing. He needed space to be allowed to do what he wanted; he needed to be out in the open with an open mind.

Stan and Jason went their separate ways. Jason needed to get up early so he'd be on the ball in the morning. It wouldn't do for him to be late, even though he'd been well and truly hustled.

He found himself smiling at a memory. Usually, he'd been the one with the upper hand on his comrades, and his secret food stash had been the largest due to the little games they'd played to occupy what little down time they'd had.

Jason heard the birds singing their dawn chorus as the sun rose slowly on the horizon. He grabbed his car keys and phone, and headed out the door. He couldn't think of anything less exciting to do than sit around the fire station all day waiting for something to happen. Tammy would have laughed if he'd told her of Stan's bet; she'd never have believed he'd actually fallen for it. He knew now that Stan was a notorious pool shark, one to be avoided unless you wanted to do something stupid like sit in a bath full of foam as one of his so-called friends had.

Tammy knew too much about these men and them about her; Jason found it bothered him increasingly. The only thing that could account for this obsession was the green-eyed monster, jealousy, who wanted to come out and play at his expense. *I'll discover your other big secret, Tammy*. His instincts told him there was something more to it than just the fire; after all, it was highly unusual for firemen to stay in touch with the people they'd rescued. She knew the whole station and they knew Toby; it was as if he belonged here. Maybe that was it; maybe Toby's father was a fireman, and Tammy was here constantly reminding him of his responsibilities, not that he could blame her if that were the case. That poor young boy deserved a father.

The next day, Jason arrived at the station exactly at nine o'clock. Stan had said he'd be there from eight o'clock on, but he had to brief the rest of the men to inform them that there'd be a civilian going along in the appliance with them on calls that day.

Jason thought it would be a good time to have a look at the engine Stan had mentioned during their game of pool. He hoped and prayed there wouldn't be any calls for him to attend; he wasn't sure he could handle a house fire, especially if there were people trapped inside, and there was nothing he could do but stand and watch. Jason shook the melancholy thoughts out of his head; perhaps they'd go to a school and show the children what to do in case of a fire.

Stan met him at the entrance and showed him around, telling him where the most important things were such as the kitchen and pool room. Jason planned to give that room a wide berth; he wasn't sure how many other pool sharks worked at the station.

'I'm curious,' he asked Stan as they walked around, 'about how you know Tammy? How did you meet her?' It bothered him that Tammy looked up to Stan; he was much older than her, and not exactly boyfriend material.

'Let's find somewhere private,' said Stan, leading him into his office. He indicated a chair. 'Sit down, Jason, and I'll tell you.' Stan had a feeling that Jason was jealous of the time Tammy spent around the firehouse. Not once had she ever shown anything other than sisterly affection for any of the people

231

working there, but Jason wouldn't know that. Since Jason had asked, it was only right to put the poor boy out of his misery, although the little boy in him wanted to drag it out a bit longer.

Jason sat down; he wasn't sure if what he was about to learn would be a good thing or not, but at least he'd finally lay this particular ghost to rest.

'I'll just go and get us both a brew before we start.' Stan left and returned a few moments later carrying coffee. He hoped the fire bell wouldn't ring, at least not until they'd finished this much-needed conversation. Stan pushed a cup towards Jason. 'Drink up. Tell me what you know about Tammy.'

'I know she survived a house fire that claimed the life of her cousin Debbie.' Well, that was true, apart from the fact that he knew about the scars on her arms and chest.

'I've been a fireman all my life. I was called in that night after one of the other lads had called in sick. Ted — I think you met him at the auction; he

232

was the one holding up the items.' Stan gave him a gentle reminder before he continued. 'Ted fought his way through the flames and went upstairs for Debbie. I went looking downstairs and found Tammy. I sincerely believe that if we'd gotten there any later, she'd have died as well.'

Stan paused and judged Jason's reaction. The young man sat there with a grim look on his face, but didn't say a word. 'It was the worst fire I'd ever seen in my entire career, and I've seen some terrible ones.'

Just the image made Jason shudder, but he sat silently, listening to Stan's tale.

'I brought her out and the ambulance took them both to the hospital, but it was too late for Debbie; she died the next day.' Stan shook his head sadly. 'Tammy and the rest of us struck up an unlikely friendship, and she's helped out at all of the fundraisers ever since.' Stan paused long enough to take a sip of his drink. 'I believe it's her way of thanking us. Usually, we get thank-you cards or a crate of beer.' Stan found it hard to judge Jason's reaction, but carried on anyway. 'We were just doing our jobs, and knowing that she is alive today is thanks enough.'

By the time Stan had finished his story, Jason's eyes had misted over at the thought of his poor, beautiful girl having to face something like that. Why hadn't he been here? Maybe he could have protected them, both of them! He still couldn't let his friends go, and he had lost another because he hadn't been there for her; instead, he'd been at war, fighting against insurgents.

'Thank you for saving her.' There was nothing else he could say; no words could express how grateful he was that Tammy had lived. No matter how he felt about her now, Jason wouldn't want anything bad to happen to her. She'd been his life for so long; just knowing she was still there was something.

Stan patted him on the shoulder. 'There's no need to thank me lad. Just make her happy.' Taking a sip of his drink, Stan continued. 'Maybe next time, it'll be you carrying a heavily pregnant lady out of a burning house. We could always use good men like you in the fire service.'

Jason's head shot up. 'What do you mean a heavily pregnant lady?'

'Lad, I had a few issues getting Tammy out; have you ever tried giving a fireman's lift to someone who's pregnant?'

Drumming his fingers on the desk, Jason sat in total silence. He felt the heat rise up the back of his neck; at least in that, she'd been telling the truth, and Stan had been there to rescue her.

'So, what's Tammy done, Jason?'

'She told me Toby was Debbie's child, and that she was bringing him up. Then a few weeks ago, she told me he was hers, and that I was Toby's dad.' Had it been that long? Two weeks since he'd seen her deep chocolate eyes? He was even missing those old-fashioned cardigans.

'I can tell from the uncertainty in your voice that you don't believe that,' replied Stan.

Jason shook his head. 'No, I don't. She wouldn't tell me how many other boyfriends she'd had. I haven't seen her since; there's no point.' He put down his cup harder than he should have done, allowing liquid to slosh over the sides. 'Let her be the one who has to live with her lies, as long as she leaves me out of it. I have enough problems of my own, trying to keep myself on the straight and narrow without being stuck with a kid who isn't mine,' snarled Jason, his tone bitter and angry.

'Look, did you ask her what her reasons were?'

'No, and I didn't give her a chance to explain either.' That was enough on this subject. 'I'd best sort that engine out,' Jason said. He got out of his chair and wandered off towards the trucks.

A few hours later, Jason was still scratching his head; he'd no idea why the engine wouldn't work properly.

He'd changed the points and the cam belt, but short of taking the whole engine apart, he couldn't think what else to do. The boys at the station were being patient with him, more so than they should. They'd had to borrow another engine from a nearby station whilst this one was out of action, leaving the other station one engine short.

The one thing that Jason loved best about the station was the camaraderie; it was similar to what he'd had in the army. He'd watched them all rush off on calls and come back happy or upset, depending on how things had gone. They couldn't always save the people, but when they did, there was a satisfaction amongst the team that Jason realised he craved. Mr Hobson had told him that, unfortunately, he didn't have any work for him up at the hall. Working on the engine was all he had now, and jobs were hard to come by, especially for an ex-squaddie. Normally, kids left school and joined up straight away, but he'd been late compared to some, so he'd have a trade to fall back on afterwards. Well, that had been the intention anyway.

Jason had had enough of this piece of scrap metal trying to punish him. Tammy had done that already. There was only one thing he hadn't checked. 'Of course, you're an idiot,' Jason said to himself as he slapped his forehead. He quickly checked the rotary arm, and there lay the problem; it wasn't one that was easy to see, but that was no excuse. *What sort of mechanic are you? Not a proper one, that's for sure,* Jason thought to himself, although he couldn't stop the laughter bubbling up inside him.

Stan would have to order the part so that he could fix it and get the engine back on the road. Then they could return the one they'd borrowed. Jason put his tools away and wiped his hands on a rag to remove most of the oil. He went to find the boss to ask him to order a new part; at least it wouldn't cost a fortune the way it would to replace a full fire engine. Jason chuckled when he found Stan playing pool by himself.

'Hey Stan, are you trying to hustle yourself?' Jason quipped.

'No, everyone else is busy doing the safety checks on the equipment, and I thought I'd grab the table. I'm sure they're planning on beating me in some sort of handicap competition.'

'Well, I can't say I blame them. Anyway, I found the problem with the engine. You need a new rotary arm; I can fix it easily, if you get the part.'

'Great! I'll phone head office and get them to sort it out. It should be here within a few days,' said Stan. 'Have you got time for a chat?'

'Sure. I'm not seeing Tammy anymore, so I have all the time you want.'

'Well,' Stan paused; he wanted to give Jason time to tell him to get lost. 'It's sort of about Tammy as well as a proposition.'

'I am not making another bet with

you over a game of pool. The odds are extremely one-sided.' Jason didn't miss the smug look on Stan's face.

'No, it's not a game of pool, but I've done something underhanded, and I hope you'll accept that I did it with the right intentions.'

'Go on, but shouldn't you be confessing to a priest?'

Stan's laughter resonated around the room. 'It's not that sort of confession.'

Jason was worried; he'd no idea what he was in for now, and with Stan, you never knew precisely where you stood. 'Okay, I'm waiting for it,' he said reluctantly.

'What are you doing this afternoon?' Stan asked.

Okay, Jason thought, *so far it doesn't seem too bad.* 'I've got no plans today,' Jason said stiffly. 'Why?'

'I want you to come with me. I'd say that I would need you for about four hours, maybe a bit longer.'

'Where are we going?'

'I thought we'd take a trip down to

headquarters to put in that order, and there is something else,' he replied mysteriously.

Okay then, so what's he doing? Jason didn't know what Stan was up to, but what he did know of his character assured him that he could be trusted. It was strange, but even on so short an acquaintance, Jason felt at ease, relaxed in his presence. The dreams hadn't returned, although his sleep pattern was erratic again.

'Sure. I've nothing better to do,' Jason replied.

They left the station and jumped into Stan's car. Headquarters was only in the next town, so it wasn't a long journey. Their footsteps echoed down the empty corridor. A sign on one of the doors read: 'Quiet please; exam in progress.'

'An exam? Stan, you want me to sit for an exam?'

Stan could see the puzzlement in Jason's face. 'Yes, just go through there, and I'll see you in a few hours.' Stan chuckled as he pushed Jason into the room; he was a good lad and the fire service needed good men like that. He'd managed to bypass the application process; he'd asked Jason's parents one day whilst Jason had been at the station to fill it in for him. Stan just wanted to get him into the exam; even if Jason passed, he'd need to pass the physical tests, and get assigned to his watch. That was providing Jason actually took the test; when he'd left, the lad had only been halfway into the room.

Part one of his plans had been put into action. Tammy would never feel insecure in her own house again; hopefully, she'd have a live-in fireman. Honestly, he was sure those two were the reason his hair had a few more strands of grey in it. Jason was a good kid, even if he were still a little messed up from his experience in the army. Their counsellor would sort him out; maybe it would be wise to have Tammy's whole family in as well. However, that could wait for another day — he had to sort this part out, get that damn engine back up and running, then go and collect Jason.

★ ★ ★

Jason exited the room fairly pleased with himself, and yet still a tad confused as to why Stan had made him take the fireman's entrance test. Just as he thought his brain would self-destruct, the man in question appeared and waltzed down the corridor without a care in the world.

'I took your exam, Stan. I'm finding it hard to decide which is worse, being hustled at pool or taking an entrance exam.'

'Well, would you have considered being a fireman without a gentle little push in the right direction?'

'No, I guess not. I didn't expect to go back into any sort of service again. I thought that if I got a job, it would be working on my own, outside some-where, not being responsible for anyone else.' The thought of his lost friends still stung, but Jason had realised he'd have to let go; his sanity depended on it. 'Is there anything else you have planned for me?'

'Mmm, well as a matter of fact, I do need to talk to you about Tammy.'

Here we go, thought Jason. Couldn't he just leave it alone? Tammy was the last person he wanted to discuss.

'I sort of know what happened, but did you give Tammy time to explain why she'd hidden Toby's existence from you?'

'Well, no. I'd heard enough when she told me he was hers and not Debbie's.' Jason paced up and down the corridor. 'What sort of person does something like that?'

'Tammy must have had her reasons for not telling you.' Stan was trying to convince Jason to give Tammy another chance. 'Let me ask you something, lad. Do you love her?'

'I don't know if I love her.' What was he doing? Trying to hide the truth from himself, or Stan? *Of course you love her*, he said to himself. 'I just don't know if I can ever trust her again,' Jason admitted reluctantly.

Stan grabbed Jason's arm so he would stop his incessant pacing. 'Jason, stop pacing up and down; you're really making me dizzy.'

Jason stopped wandering up and down the corridor and stared Stan straight in the eye.

'If I were you, I'd at least give her a chance to explain, and allow her to give you her reasons,' said Stan.

'I just don't know. Is this why you made me take that exam?' Jason didn't know what Stan had hoped to accomplish. He still had to go through a physical and basic training before he qualified. Was that what he really wanted? To help people? It was all he'd done for years, but he didn't want to feel useless, to know he wasn't good enough for anything. Jason knew his leg would heal fully; it would just take time. He was fit and healthy, and the blokes at the station were decent men. 'Don't answer that, Stan. I will, if I've passed that entrance test. I'll be able to join you all down at the station.' Jason realised that Stan was giving him a chance to make something of himself, to know that he could be relied upon — and most importantly, make it so that he could believe in himself again.

'Well, let's go and celebrate,' said Stan. 'Do me a favour, though, and think about what I said. Will you give Tammy a chance to explain?' Stan patted him on the back and led him out of headquarters.

'I guess I'll need to get a uniform,' Jason added as they crossed the car park to Stan's car.

'Don't worry about that, lad; there are plenty of them in the stores.' Stan tried to hide his smile. Part one of his plan was definitely working. He hoped Tammy and Toby would be happy with the new improved Jason. Stan knew that the two of them were so right for each other; it was a pity the two love birds hadn't realised it themselves yet.

Stan wasn't sure how he could bring them together. Tammy would have turned and run away from the idea. From what Jason had told him, Tammy had lied to him; but by the sound of it, she'd be too scared to do anything about that now. She'd finally told him the truth, but Jason had got angry. At this moment, Stan was extremely disappointed in Tammy; she really shouldn't have expected anything less. The poor bloke was in a state already, and she'd made it worse. He wanted to give her a piece of his mind.

10

Tammy held onto Toby's hand as they entered the local corner shop. She couldn't face the hustle and bustle of the supermarket; after all, she only needed bread and milk. It would cost more in petrol just to get there. The corner shop was the farthest she had been in a few days. It was unlikely that Jason would be out shopping for his mum, but she wasn't going to take a chance on bumping into him. She saw it as another good reason to avoid the supermarket and shop locally.

Toby walked quietly by her side; unusual for him, she thought. Toby was normally so chatty and active. For the past few days, he seemed to mope around listlessly, constantly saying he was bored. Toby had even refused to watch *Duck Tales*, which was a shock. He loved that programme more than any other cartoon. Tammy had initially put it down to illness, but now she wasn't so sure; he had shown no signs of having a cold or anything else.

'What's wrong, darling?' Tammy asked him.

Toby shrugged his shoulders in reply. *Well I'm not going to get a lot out of you, am I?* she thought.

He'd hardly spoken to her in the last few days. Unless she asked him a question, or he flung himself down on the settee telling her how bored he was, most of the time Toby didn't even acknowledge her presence. As Tammy reached the till with the few purchases she'd made, she overheard Mrs Ashworth talking.

'I'm so worried about Eric Clayton; he wasn't at the tea dance on Tuesday afternoon down at the community centre.'

Tammy's brow knitted together. Eric Clayton had done administrative work for the fire station before he retired. He was like a grandfather to all the men, as were all the old servicemen that lived in the bungalows.

'Excuse me, Mrs Ashworth. I'm so sorry for eavesdropping, but I heard you said you hadn't seen Eric in a few days. Have you been round?' Tammy enquired.

'Aye, young 'un, but I didn't get a reply. It's very rude of him not to answer the door; I won't go again,' she replied through thin lips.

Tammy was concerned. She knew Eric hadn't any family to speak of. From what she remembered, he'd never married and had always lived on his own.

'I'll go round to his house and see if he'll open the door. Perhaps he's caught a chill and isn't well.' The concern grew inside Tammy. Taking her phone out of her pocket, she tapped a message out asking her mum to have Toby. She supposed that Eric was due to dance with Mrs Ashworth on Tuesday, and he'd stood her up. That wasn't the Eric she knew. He was very regimented, always neat and tidy, and always punctual. He hated anyone being late. There was something wrong, seriously wrong. She could phone him, but what if he couldn't answer?

'Do you want to come with me? I can get the master key to the fireman's bungalows from Stan.'

Mrs Ashworth wagged her finger. 'No, and you can tell that Eric Clayton it's the last time I save him a dance.' Mrs Ashworth pulled on Tammy's sleeve. 'Well, if he is ill, it was still very inconsiderate of him.'

'I'll tell him.' Tammy had to suppress a giggle. She felt Mrs Ashworth was acting like a spoilt child; but then again, she doubted very much that it would feel nice to be stood up and unable to dance. She smiled indulgently at her, made cursory goodbye remarks, and dashed off.

Toby trailed along behind her, his bottom lip still threatening to trip him up. She didn't turn round and tell Mrs Ashworth that sometimes, someone was so ill they couldn't let anyone know. It reminded her not to cross the dear lady, or else she would be the one feeling the sharp end of her tongue. She did want to laugh, though, the more she thought about it, but she decided that this wouldn't be a good thing to do.

Tammy hated the thought of anyone alone or helpless, especially one of the men from the station. She called Stan and gave him a garbled message. Stan agreed to meet her at Eric's house in an hour, once he got rid of the fire inspectors. Tammy wanted to go around beforehand, but this would give her ample time to leave Toby with her mother.

Although her mother said they were going out, she agreed to take Toby with them, freeing her up to go and see why Mr Clayton hadn't been seen on Tuesday, and why he hadn't contacted anyone. Tammy was worried; she wouldn't want to live on her own with no one to rely on. When you got to a certain age, things became a bit more difficult.

'You're going to stay at Grandma's for a few hours, Toby.'

'Why can't I stay with Jason?'

'You can't,' Tammy replied, exasperated.

'But why?'

'Enough, Toby.' Tammy hardly ever lost her temper with her son, but now at least she knew the reason for his bad mood. He was missing Jason just as she was. Unfortunately, there was nothing she could do about it. For a few short days, Jason had been a big part of her life and Toby's, and because she hadn't told the truth from the word go, karma was definitely paying her back.

She dropped Toby off and started the short walk around to Mr Clayton's bungalow. The curtains were still closed and there were newspapers sticking out of the letterbox. Tammy looked around; Stan was nowhere to be seen. It didn't look good; Eric always opened his curtains and would never leave the papers that way.

At that moment, Tammy hated herself. Why hadn't she called round? *You were too busy with your own life to worry about other people*. The voice in her head was back like a bad penny or a nasty household smell that lingered forever.

She walked around the side of the house. The gate was locked, and it wasn't one that she would be able to climb over easily. As energetic as she was, scaling six-foot fences wasn't her forte. Taking her phone out, she rang Eric's house phone. She heard it ringing, but no one answered. The hairs on the back of her neck stood on end; there was definitely something wrong. Where was Stan? Just as she was about to curse his tardiness, the man in question shouted her name.

'Tammy!'

When she heard her name being called, she hurried around to the front of the house. 'Stan, I'm so glad you came. I've just tried ringing him, but there's no answer. The newspapers are hanging out of the letterbox. The curtains are shut, and . . . ' she said without pausing for a breath.

Stan dismissed the pleasantries and his usual greeting. 'Calm down; I'm here now,' he said as he opened the door with the master key. Once the door was opened, they both entered and ran off in different directions. Tammy raced upstairs whilst Stan checked downstairs.

'Eric?' Tammy waited for a reply. Silence. All of a sudden, she heard a faint cry. Damn! The bedrooms were empty; the only place she hadn't checked was the bathroom. Tammy pushed the handle down with great force, but the door was locked from the inside. Placing her ear to the door, she shouted Eric's name again. The muffled voice came from inside the room.

'Stan, Eric's in the bathroom.'

Heavy footsteps on the stairs alerted Tammy that Stan was on his way. 'Tammy, move.'

Tammy moved to the other end of the hallway. She watched as Stan kicked the door several times, his hands gripping the railing and the door frame. After a few more kicks, he gained access to the bathroom. Eric lay on the floor, shivering, and sporting a large cut and bruise to his forehead.

Tammy rushed forward. 'Eric, are you all right?' Her tears threatened to spill; she had no idea what would have happened if they hadn't gotten there in time. Leaving Eric alone and helpless — what sort of people were they? No one had said anything to her, so how was she supposed to know?

'I fell.' His eyes were wide with a mixture of fear and relief. Tammy folded a towel and placed it gently under his head. She ran into his bedroom, dragged the duvet off his bed, and ran back into the bathroom where she placed it gently over him. She thought it would warm him up; at least, she hoped it would.

'I'm going to phone for the ambulance.' Stan's voice caught in his throat, and it held relief and anguish.

They'd have to make sure they hired a warden; that way there'd be someone to check on people seven days a week. Tammy hoped Stan could implement that, so all the residents would feel safe. 'Okay, Stan.' She filled the glass sitting on the side of the sink. Kneeling beside Eric, she brought it to his mouth allowing him to drink the cool, refreshing liquid.

'Help me up,' Eric commanded.

Tammy smiled at him; no wonder his voice was so low. His mouth must be very dry.

'I can't, Eric; you need to stay there and wait for the ambulance to come.' She reached for his hand. 'When did you fall?'

'I was getting ready for the tea dance; I had a date with Mrs Ashworth.' There was a twinkle of mischief in his eyes.

'I'm so sorry that I didn't come round sooner.' Tammy was absolutely devastated; it was a good job they'd arrived when they did. Eric might not have made it if he had been left any longer lying on the cold bathroom floor without food and unable to get water.

'Oh hush, lassie. It doesn't matter. I'm just glad you're here now.' Eric smiled weakly.

'Mrs Ashworth was angry when you didn't show up, and that's what prompted me to come around.' Tammy's eyes drifted around the avocado-coloured bathroom. This might have been the height of fashion in the seventies, but it was definitely outdated now.

'You remind me so much of a nurse I once knew,' Eric replied.

'Oh?' Tammy didn't really know what to say.

'Aye, it was the Battle of Anzio!'

Tammy wasn't sure what that had to do with his fall. Perhaps he'd hit his head too hard and was conjuring up images from the past.

'I'd recently turned 18. I'd only just

finished basic training.' Eric seemed to want to talk, but his voice was becoming quiet and barely audible. Tammy lifted the glass up to his lips and allowed him to take another few sips of water. Stan reappeared in the doorway.

'Is the ambulance on its way?' Tammy asked. Stan merely nodded his head.

She turned her attention back to Eric. 'So you were telling me about your army days.' Tammy thought it was best to keep him talking; she didn't want him losing consciousness. She didn't really know what she was doing; she only wanted to keep talking to him and make him comfortable until help arrived. Stan was on standby, and he hadn't said she was doing anything wrong. He'd checked Eric's heart and pulse, and everything seemed fine in those areas.

'I'd not been in the service long when we were sent to Italy and Anzio.' A sadness entered Eric's voice.

'You don't have to talk now, Eric. There will be plenty of time for that.' Tammy tried to sooth the old gentleman.

'I'd rather talk. I've not spoken to anyone in days,' Eric replied.

Tammy felt terrible. She couldn't imagine what it had been like to be alone in the house for days without someone to talk to, lying helpless on a cold bathroom floor.

What would have happened if she hadn't overheard Mrs Ashworth's comment about the tea dance? How would anyone have known that there was something wrong? Why didn't people look out for their neighbours anymore like they had in the old days? She supposed it was because everyone was too busy with their own lives to bother about anyone else. No one really knew their neighbours today, so people must have thought it best to mind their own business and keep to themselves.

'Now, where was I?' Eric muttered more to himself than to anyone else.

'Anzio, that was it. I'd just joined the army after basic training, and we were sent off to the shores of Italy and Anzio.' Eric looked thoughtful for a moment. 'We had to get up on the beach and into the town.'

Tammy smiled indulgently, but didn't comment. If it meant keeping Eric awake, she'd listen to anything, but the last thing she really wanted to hear was an army story.

'You know, we surprised the Jerrys all right. They didn't know we were coming. They didn't even have a skeleton crew protecting that beach.' Eric seemed to gasp for breath. 'I never made it off the beach that day.'

Tammy looked towards Stan and then back at Eric. She couldn't understand why he'd made a statement like that. She held the glass up to his lips again and made him drink some more, despite his protests to the contrary.

Eric grinned. 'You look shocked, little one.'

Tammy believed that if he'd been feeling a hundred percent, he'd be rubbing his hands together since he had her totally confused.

'There weren't many people injured on that first day. Unfortunately, I was one of them.' He weakly raised his right hand. 'Made a good job of it, didn't they?' He made sure she could see the leather glove which was now his arm. He never took his glove off and always hid it inside his pocket, not wanting people to see. Eric had always thought it was better to have people think his own arm had been injured beyond repair than to let them know he wore a false one.

Tammy was speechless. She turned to Stan, but saw that this hadn't surprised him. He'd obviously known all along about Eric's injury. If Tammy were totally honest with herself, she'd thought Eric had had a stroke. Although she paid attention to the people in the bungalows and checked on them every so often, she didn't spend much time there. Eric enjoyed seeing the shocked look on Tammy's face.

'I had to learn to do everything left-handed — paint, eat, dress myself. I even managed to get a job doing administrative work at the fire station.'

Tammy knew that many people had died during the war and that it was meant to end all wars; pity that idea hadn't worked out.

'I can't believe you're so cheerful about it all.'

'No, don't misunderstand me, lassie. Having this happen to you when you're just 18 changes your life forever. Instead of curling up in a corner and licking my wounds, I got up and carried on. I told myself many others died, and I was still here to tell my tale.' Eric patted her hand. 'Here in England, people died during the blitz, but none of them gave up, Tammy. You're too good to lock yourself in a tower away from the world.'

Tammy didn't know what to say. Had

she been that obvious? She thought she'd been pretty clever, hiding the pain and hurt she'd felt, but perhaps she hadn't been as clever as she believed, especially if people could see straight through it.

Jason had said the same; he'd survived. She thought he was just trying to make her feel better, but maybe he'd actually been trying to tell her something after all. One lesson she'd learned from Eric's story was that she'd made the biggest mistake of her life in keeping Toby a secret from him. The truth would have been preferable to a web of lies and deceit that had resulted in nothing but the loss of someone special.

Was Jason someone special to her even now? Absentmindedly, she touched her mouth, remembering the way he had kissed her. The day they'd spent together in the park with Toby ran through her mind; it had been one of the best days she'd had in a long time. Everything that had happened since then was changing her outlook on life. What did people say? *Carpe diem!* That was it: seize the day. Tammy knew it was her turn to seize the day with everything she had, and to grab hold of the happiness she craved. Was it too late? Only time would tell.

'Your young man is hurting; I saw that haunted look in the eyes of the soldiers in the field hospital, whilst they fixed me hand. He needs someone like you, someone kind and caring. Look after him.' Eric closed his eyes.

'Eric, don't go to sleep. Stay awake,' Tammy pleaded. She wasn't going to let anything happen to him, not now. This time, she'd help someone who needed it.

'Oh, stop fussing.' Eric said crossly. He hated anyone mollycoddling him. 'The lights hurting me eyes,' he complained.

Stan switched the bathroom light off, whilst Tammy pulled the blind halfway down the window.

'I'm not going anywhere. The Jerry

didn't get me, and I'm not going to let a fall stop me either,' he barked.

Tammy breathed a sigh of relief, but did wonder how he knew about Jason. Then it came to her. Eric had been at the auction and would've seen them together. It always made her laugh. A person saw you with someone for the first time and automatically assumed you were a couple. *You could have been but for your own stupidity*, she chastised herself. The sound of approaching sirens alerted her to the ambulance's arrival.

'I'll go to the hospital with him,' Stan said.

Stan went to escort the paramedics into the house. Eric would be all right now, and he was happy about that. There could be no repeat performances of this; no one was going to be allowed to fall and hurt themselves and be left alone and unnoticed. He'd heard of too many people dying alone from injuries, or just because their bodies have given up.

Tammy had almost forgotten Stan had been there; he'd stood quietly in the doorway while Eric had told his story. She'd been left with a lot to consider. The horrors of war hadn't affected Eric as they had Jason. Perhaps it had been because Eric had only seen one day of action, as he put it, but both had had their lives irrevocably changed by enlisting. Two people with similar circumstances had to cope with horrors beyond what most people could imagine. Tammy wasn't sure what Eric had been trying to tell her, but she knew she'd figure it out later.

It was too late to say 'sorry' to Jason. He didn't want to know anything; he'd walked out of her life for good, and even Toby was upset at her for it. Well, she couldn't really blame him. After all, what could a four-year-old actually understand? Someone had come into his life briefly, and then had gone away again. It was a bit like a favourite teacher at nursery; you have them for a while, then you get someone new.

Tammy moved out of the way to let the paramedics do their job. 'I can go with him, Stan.'

'No, you need to get back to Toby. I said I'd go. My shift has finished and I feel some responsibility; I never came to check up on him myself.'

Tammy didn't miss the guilty look in his eye. It had been nobody's fault, but they knew now to be more vigilant. She had an idea about panic buttons that people wore around their necks or pinned to their clothing. If anything happened, someone would be there almost instantly. The trustees of the bungalows would have to agree, but Tammy didn't see that as being a problem.

Tammy texted her parents; she wasn't sure if they'd returned from Brighton yet. She received an answer almost instantly. They'd decided to stay a while longer and weren't sure when they'd be coming home. She opted to go and wait for Stan at the fire station. She didn't really want to be alone, not today. Perhaps Toby would come home in a better mood after being with her parents. She wasn't sure if she could cope with his attitude, especially after the day she'd had.

★ ★ ★

Jason was at a total loss; he missed spending time with Tammy, her silly grin, and her wacky over-the-top clothes. He missed the breakfasts she used to make him and the way she melted into his arms. He missed watching cartoons with Toby, playing with his toy fire engines, and the play fights they'd had. For a short time he'd had a family, but now it was gone.

Jason had driven around to Tammy's parents' house; he'd agreed to do the rest of the painting today, and the morning was already half gone. He couldn't help but wonder if Toby would be there. He'd come to love everything that Toby did. The child was innocent and saw each and everything as one big

adventure. Could a child bring someone so much happiness? He had heard
that people said so, but could it be true?

Jason knocked on the door and
waited. When the door opened, Mrs
Morgan stood there with her outdoor
coat, her husband and Toby right
behind her. 'I've come to finish off the
rest of the work,' Jason said.

'Jason, I had totally forgot you were
coming today. We're just off to Brighton. Mr Morgan needs to see the
solicitor about purchasing a new
warehouse.'

Jason felt his face fall. 'Oh, OK, I can
come back another day.'

'I've got an idea. Why don't you take
our Toby onto Brighton Pier? Solicitors'
offices are so dreary for children,' Mrs
Morgan suggested.

Jason jumped at the chance. He was
glad to have the opportunity to spend
the day with Toby, without Tammy or
her parents around. It was lucky she
didn't know that he had Toby and not
her mum and dad. By the sound of

things, she'd something important to do and they had to go out. Now, he was happily riding his motorbike into Brighton.

He recalled the time he had taken Tammy to the pier. Brighton Pier had been opened in the nineteenth century and had entertained people with all its delights and the sound of waves crashing around the pillars. The scent of vinegar mixed with candy floss filled Jason's nostrils and made his stomach rumble.

'Toby, what do you want to go on first? Or are you hungry?' Jason asked.

Taking Jason's hand, Toby dragged him to where he wanted to go, his arm stretched out pointing to the brightly coloured trampolines. 'I think the trampolines; that looks like fun.'

Jason wasn't sure. 'I told your Grandma I wouldn't let anything happen to you.'

Toby let out a deep breath. 'Mum and Grandma worry too much; I told you that already, didn't I? Come on, I want to go on there.' He added a 'please' just to keep Jason sweet.

'Just like your mum! You always seem to get your own way.' Laughing loudly, Jason paid the operator for one go for Toby. He watched happily as the boy squealed with delight, bouncing up and down. A little girl took Toby's hand, and they bounced together.

The smell of fish and chips was making Jason hungry. Brightly coloured stands were everywhere he turned, making his belly growl. Toby came running over to him, shouting, 'Jason that was so much fun! Can I go on again?'

Jason smiled. 'Don't you want to go on a few other things first? I don't know about you, but the 'Horror Hotel' looks good.' As soon as he had suggested it, he regretted the idea. That amusement was probably too scary for a four-year-old. Suddenly, Jason felt he was drowning; he hadn't any experience with kids. Knowing what was the right thing or wrong thing to do, especially in regards to entertaining them, was something totally alien to him.

'Come on, then,' Toby said. 'I'll look after you, if you find it too scary, Jason.'

They both laughed. Hand-in-hand, they made their way round to the next ride. Climbing into the car, Jason kept a tight hold on the shiny metal bar, so it didn't come loose. He wasn't going to risk an accident, especially with Tammy's son. There was no way Tammy would be able to cope if anything ever happened to him. It looked as though she'd barely held herself together over the last few years.

Creepy pop music played in the background, as ghosts and spider webs dropped down in front of the bright yellow car. Toby squealed with a mix of fright and excitement at every turn. Jason found his hand being squeezed harder and harder as the ride continued, until a bright beam of light blazed in front of them pointing to the end of the ride.

As the car halted, Toby spoke. 'Jason,

that's the scariest thing I've ever seen. Can we go on it again?'

They climbed out of the car and dashed around the barriers, rejoining the back of the queue for another go on the 'Horror House'. 'What colour this time, Toby?' Jason asked.

'Mmm, the red one,' he said with enthusiasm.

Jason smiled indulgently at Toby. Could this really be his son? No matter what had happened, he was happy he could share this little bundle of joy. Jason made his mind up about one thing: Toby wouldn't be joining the armed forces. He'd be a fireman instead.

Each time Toby came off a ride, he asked if he could go on it again. Jason found the repetition a tad annoying, but he chastised himself, reminding himself that here was a young child out for some fun. He had no right to be annoyed if Toby asked him to go on anything more than once.

'Let's go get ice cream and some

food, then you can choose something else to go on,' Jason said.

Toby held out his hand for Jason. They walked up to the first fish and chip stall.

'Do you like fish, Toby?'

'Oh yes, and I like chips too, but don't tell Mummy. I'm not allowed to eat them.' Toby placed his finger to his lips.

What child wouldn't be allowed to eat chips? He was gobsmacked. How could anyone ban a food from their child? Then, like an eagle swooping down on its prey, it hit him — chips! Of course! Tammy wouldn't give them to him; it would mean having a chip pan in the house.

Jason took him over to the various stalls scattered around. He wanted to buy Toby a present, but although there were plenty of cuddly toys, he didn't think they would be suitable for the little lad. Just as he was about to give up, he spotted a bright red and yellow fire helmet with an outfit to match.

Jason smiled inwardly to himself as he rushed towards the stall. He didn't need to point out the outfit since Toby had already seen it.

'Jason, look at that.' His eyes opened wide with surprise and awe.

'Would you like it, Toby?'

Jason didn't really need to ask; he already knew the answer to that. What little boy, mad about fire engines, wouldn't want a fireman suit? It even had a little pretend hose attached to the belt. Jason paid for the suit, and kneeling down in front of his son, he handed it to him. Toby flung his arms around his neck and squeezed him tightly. Tears pricked the back of Jason's eyes. A new-found love for his son poured out of him at this simple gesture of unconditional love.

'Just wait till Mummy sees me in this. Jason, please can I put it on now?'

'Come on, let's go and find somewhere you can put it on.' Jason found a quiet spot at the end of the pier. Toby wasted no time in ripping off the packaging, leaving it strewn all over the wooden boards. Jason helped him into the suit and put the helmet on his head. He took out his phone and took a picture. *That will make a better wallpaper design*, he thought.

'Pick up your rubbish, Toby; you can't leave it lying around. The birds might hurt themselves.'

Without question, Toby did as he was asked and placed it all in the rubbish bin. He did look rather smart in his new outfit. He wondered what Tammy would say if she knew he had been with Toby for most of the day. Would she object to his looking after him? He was still in one piece, and by the sound of his chatter and high-pitched squeak each time he went on a ride, it was obvious little Toby was enjoying himself.

The morning sped by too quickly for Jason's liking. It might be a long time before he'd see him again, and he wanted to make as much of the time as he possibly could. They slowly wandered to the end of the pier, where he'd arranged to meet Mr and Mrs Morgan, although he desperately wanted to keep Toby a bit longer. He'd like to think that the next day and every day after, he'd have a chance to repeat the fun they'd had together — not necessarily at the seaside, but going to the park, or reading a bedtime story.

'Come on, I have to get you back,' Jason sighed reluctantly.

Toby stamped his foot and folded his arms. 'But Jason! None of the rides have shut. Why we have to go now? I'm having so much fun.'

'I know, but I have to get you back before it gets too late. Besides, it will take at least an hour for your grandma and granddad to drive home.'

With a lot of huffing and puffing, Toby eventually agreed. Jason was overcome with the sadness that washed over him like a tidal wave; his time had run out. Maybe it was his subconscious telling him that there was something about this little boy that was necessary to him. He felt comfortable in his presence; the way they had snuggled on the sofa that day had been so natural, as if they'd known each other all his young life. Now, he understood why he'd been feeling like that. Maybe he could get Tammy to agree to let him have Toby each weekend, instead of for a few hours once in a blue moon.

Jason wondered if Tammy thought of him every now and again. She'd been ingrained in his heart and mind for so long, that thinking of her felt as natural as breathing to him. Mr and Mrs Morgan stood at the end of the pier, and Jason waved to them to let them know he'd seen them.

'Hey, honey.' Mrs Morgan picked up her grandson and swung him around. 'Did you have a good time?'

'It was wicked! I wanted to stay, but Jason said we had to go.'

Jason saw Tammy's parents look at one another. 'How about we drive to the adventure playground for a bit?'

Jason nodded. He wasn't quite ready to let go of Toby yet. He hadn't mentioned the lies Tammy had told him, pretending that he was Toby's father. It wouldn't have been right to get the child's hopes up.

'Can I go with Jason?' Toby pleaded.

'No, he's on a bike, Toby. You come with us and Jason will meet us there.'

'Will you buy me an ice cream?' the child asked Jason.

Jason caught the look of horror in Mrs Morgan's face. 'That's rude, Toby; you should wait to be asked and not demand things. Jason has already been more than kind to you today.'

Toby's head went down, and reluctantly Toby walked off with his grandparents and Jason jumped on his new bike. He'd been amazed that, after only a few short hours, Toby had come to mean a lot to him. Jason tried to reason it out, but it seemed impossible to do so.

The bike ride hadn't cleared his head like he'd hoped it would. If he was ever troubled before, he'd go for a long drive in the country, and it would usually help. As Jason pulled into Brookland's car park, he saw that the others were already there.

'Come on, mate,' Mr Morgan shouted, waving him over to them. 'We've been waiting for you.'

'I needed a ride, sorry.' He strolled over to them.

Mr Morgan slapped him on the back. 'Did it clear your head?'

'No, a drive usually does. I don't know what is wrong with me lately; nothing seems to be going right.'

'Jason, you're going to have to snap out of it for the day, mate.' Tammy's father looked pointedly at his wife and grandson. 'You are a good lad, Jason and you know I am here for you, if you ever need to talk.'

Jason shook his head. Mr Morgan was right; whatever it was that had upset him would have to take a back seat while Toby was around. Jason thought Toby looked familiar, but for the life of him, he couldn't place him. Try as he might, he couldn't put his finger on the person the child resembled. Apart from being of slight build, he didn't look like Tammy at all. *Oh, stop over-thinking things; just have fun and pretend to be a child again*, he chastised himself.

'Toby, do you want an ice cream now?' he asked.

Toby thought about it for a moment and then replied, 'No, thank you. I know a secret.'

Curiosity got the best of Jason. Toby did seem quite keen on letting out the family secrets.

'You really shouldn't tell a secret. That's why they're called secrets.' Jason looked at him, but deep down he hoped Toby would give up whatever piece of information he had; maybe it would help him.

'Mummy has a photo of you. Let's go on the swings now.'

Toby grabbed Jason by the hand and dragged him towards the swings. His grandparents strolled arm-in-arm behind them.

Jason's heart soared; maybe she didn't hate him quite as much as he thought she did. *No, Jason, you shouldn't read too much into things. Calm down. It could just be a photo of the old gang; after all, we were always taking pictures.*

Looking at Mrs Morgan, he raised his eyebrow, but she didn't take the bait. *Can't trust you can I?* Jason said to himself. Tammy's parents weren't prepared to give anything away. *I wonder what other revelations will be made today?* Jason realised he could be reading too much into things.

'I'll bet you can't beat me to the swings, Toby.' Jason set off jogging. As he looked back, he saw Toby had joined him in the game. He slowed down to a walking pace, so Toby would beat him and win the impromptu race.

Jumping up and down, Toby screamed. 'I won! I beat you, ha ha ha!'

Toby's laughter was infectious, as was

his personality; he seemed to have the ability to lift Jason's spirits without even trying. Would it matter if he just let him have a go on his bike? He didn't have to have the engine running; he'd just wheel it around. Jason thought he'd best ask Mr Morgan first. When he received a positive answer, Jason walked Toby over to his new custom-built Kawasaki. He sat him on it but refused Toby's pleas to move the bike anywhere. After all, if something should happen to him, Jason would be the first one Tammy would blame, and that wouldn't be a good thing. Jason loved the smile on Toby's face as he pretended to ride the bike. How much alike they were, just the way Toby looked, which reminded Jason of a photograph his parents had of him when he was small.

Tammy arrived at the park to pick up Toby. She had to see him after Eric's accident; she felt she needed to be close to her son. It was strange that her parents had taken him to Brighton and then the park, unless they had wanted an uninterrupted night, and not have to watch *Duck Tales* for the hundredth time. Toby would be too tired to do anything except sleep.

As Tammy turned the corner into the park, she was struck by a constant buzzing noise which seemed to be following her. Quickly turning round to see what was making the awful noise, she was horrified to see a wasp flying around her head. Tammy ran as fast as she could, flailing her arms around her head trying to get it off her. Seeing her parents up ahead she ran faster, turning to look behind her, screeching and screaming at the horrible creature. If there was one thing that she couldn't abide, it was wasps. Tammy ran around in circles, wafting her hands through her hair trying to escape.

Jason stood hidden by a tree but he had a clear view of Tammy's antics. He wanted to laugh out loud. She looked ridiculous but beautiful at the same time. He could hear his heart pounding against his chest. He heard Toby's musical laughter as the little boy looked to his mum. When Tammy eventually reached them she tripped over a fallen branch and lay sprawled on the concrete path.

'Tam, what on earth are you doing?' Jason asked as he stepped into view.

'Jason.' The shocked look on her face was a picture.

Holding out his hand, he helped Tammy to her feet. 'I . . . '

Tammy's mum stepped in before he had chance to finish. 'Jason took Toby onto the pier and came here to the park with us.' Mrs Morgan sighed, 'It's time you told him Tammy. To see them together is how it should be.'

Jason looked shocked. 'Mrs Morgan. If it's about Toby, he isn't — he can't be — '

'Jason dear, if your still unsure, look at Toby — the way he stands, sits and eats. He even looks the same as you did many years ago,' she said reassuringly.

Jason looked from Tammy to her

mother and they both nodded their heads. Mr Morgan had taken Toby a little distance away. 'But, you said?'

'I'm so sorry Jason. I cannot give you any reason as to why I said what I did.'

'I can't deal with this now.' Jason walked briskly over to Toby and said his goodbyes before speeding off on his bike.

Tammy decided it was best to come clean with Toby, especially with Jason having taken him out today. He still didn't believe her, but he might believe what her mum had said, and all she could do was be there when Jason wanted to ask questions. A dark thought crossed her mind. What if he wanted to take Toby away from her?

'Come here, darling,' she shouted as she sat on a park bench. Her son ran over to her and, picking him up, she sat him on her knee. Tammy took a deep breath 'Listen Toby, you know what you've always wanted?'

She saw her son's eyes widen. 'A daddy?'

'Well . . .' Tammy paused, the words catching in her throat. 'I know how you have always wanted to have a daddy.' Tammy was finding it all very difficult, and parroting her son's response wasn't the best thing to do. 'Jason is your daddy. He has been in the army. Jason is a soldier. That is why he hasn't been here.' Tammy held her breath as she waited for all the tears and the tantrums, but none came. Well at least it was partly true; he had been in the army. 'He loves you very much.' Tammy wasn't sure how true that statement was, but at least it was better than saying she wasn't sure if Jason cared about him.

'That's cool, mummy. My new Daddy can take me out and buy me toys.'

She squeezed him tight. 'I'm sure he will, darling. I'm sure he will.'

Toby was staying with her parents again tonight. What she really wanted to do was to hide away. Jason trying to take Toby away was a real possibility,

288

and it looked like he was here to stay. Her well-used methods might not work anymore, but how far from her could she push him?

11

Tammy scrubbed the kitchen floor as if her life depended on it. Whenever she was worried or anxious she would clean, and usually it was the kitchen floor that would be scrubbed. *Just call me Cinderella*, Tammy thought. At least floors didn't talk back to her. There was nothing else she could do; she had ruined everything. Jason would never forgive her now. The reasons she had for hiding Toby's existence from him didn't hold up anymore. He had seen her scars, seen how Debbie's death had affected her; and yet despite how much he had come to mean to both of them, she had continued her deception about her son. His son. When she really should have come forward and explained her reasons. There was such venom in his words; he had slammed the door shut behind him, vowing to have Toby whenever he chose.

Why did I ever say what I did? The truth would have hurt him, but not as much as this. A knock at the door stopped her in her tracks. *Great, who's this?* she thought. *Someone else here to give me a piece of their mind. I've had enough. I just want to be left alone. Doesn't anyone understand that?* Tammy hesitated at the door.

'Jason.' Tammy was shocked he had even bothered to come round.

'Can I come in?' He was wearing a fireman's uniform. What was he doing wearing that? Was it something he had done for Toby?

'I don't want you here.' Tammy's voice squeaked as panic set in. Holding the door only slightly open, she didn't want him just walking in, demanding anything, especially not Toby. 'Jason, Toby is my son and if you think that you're just going to waltz back into my life demanding anything you want, then you have another thing coming.' She would protect her child with her last breath.

Jason stuck his foot in the door. 'Tammy, you owe me an explanation. It's the very least you can do.'

Tammy wanted to close the door in his face and hide. He had every right to be angry at her. Luckily he hadn't gone and questioned anyone else about Toby. The whole town knew he had been hers all along, and how many people had Jason told that she had lied? Would she be able to walk down the street without people whispering behind her back? She realised that Jason wasn't going to leave until he got the answers he wanted.

'So, are you going to let me in? Or we can have this conversation right here, if that's what you want.'

'Toby's not here.' She could barely get her words out.

'I don't believe you. Let me check,' he demanded.

'Go around to my mother's and ask her to see Toby, if you don't believe me, because he's there.' Tammy started to push the door closed again but it stuck on his foot. She hadn't seen him doing that. She needed to put some distance between them. Tammy wasn't prepared for a fight and she needed to gather her strength before she faced him. She still wanted to stick to her previous resolution but her body ached for him.

'No, I came to see you. We need to talk and I don't want to argue with you. I didn't want Toby here, that's all.'

Tammy did think it was high time she told him the truth — the whole truth, leaving nothing out this time. They walked into the living room in silence, and for several minutes neither said anything. Tammy held back the tears that threatened to overflow; she couldn't lose Toby, not now. She could see Jason's hands clenched tightly by his sides as she allowed him into the living room.

'Tell me why you kept it a secret from me? Please Tammy, you owe me that much.' Jason paused and then continued, 'Why is it one minute I think I've got close to you and the next you're pushing me away?'

Tammy saw that his face was a mixture of pain and love, but instead of answering him she walked out of the living room to retrieve the things she had kept all these years. Heading upstairs to her bedroom, she picked up the pile of photo albums and DVDs from the dresser which she had made for Jason. After Debbie's funeral she had made several of the two of them together; it helped her to remember all the good times that she and Debbie had shared, from their days at nursery to the high school prom. Her mum said it would help. Tammy had to agree it had helped a little, although nothing could replace the guilt she felt that Debbie wasn't still there with her.

Tammy had tried to delude herself that Jason would never know he was a father, but things as big as this have a way of being known. She started to make albums of Toby too, a scrapbook of memories. Her own albums contained the same pictures as the ones for Jason. When Toby was older and she was no longer there, his would contain happy childhood memories of his mum. Tammy knew that photographs, although nice to look at, would in no way replace the time Jason had lost with his son. Toby was four and in all that time he didn't know he had a father, or even what they did. All his friends would have dads who came to the plays or fêtes that his nursery had, and he just had her. Opening one of the albums, she saw a picture of Toby in a bedside incubator, a solitary tear dripped onto the page. Tammy looked at a few pictures and thought about all the things they could have shared if he hadn't left her to go into the army.

Tammy knew she could have stopped him, but didn't she let Jason go and do what he needed to do? Toby had looked so cute dressed as an angel for the nursery nativity play. His tinsel wings and halo kept falling down, so she'd had to use hairgrips to keep it in place. She couldn't replace all the firsts Jason had missed, but he wouldn't have to miss anything else. She would give in to his demands and let him see his son whenever he wanted. Bringing herself back to the present, Tammy couldn't allow regrets to get in the way. She had let him go without a fight. Even though it hurt her to bring Toby up alone, she believed at the time it was the right thing to do.

Each time Toby had achieved anything it went within the pages of the album, captured as a memory forever — his first tentative steps or his first day at nursery; the first time he rode his trike around the patio. Tammy had done everything alone; there was no one with whom she could share the joy, either her best friend or Toby's dad.

'I've got something for you,' she said as she handed Jason her precious cargo. 'There's lots of photos of Toby and some DVDs of when he took his first steps. I thought you might like them.'

'I'm glad you did, and thank you. It means a lot to me that you even thought of doing these.' He placed the albums down on the coffee table.

Jason held his hand on hers for a few seconds; Tammy could feel the electrical charge running between them. 'I wanted to tell you about the pregnancy.' Tammy's shoulders tensed. 'I mean . . . ' She had lost the words. 'Then when you wanted to join the army . . . Sometimes things need to stay hidden.'

'This wasn't some secret!' Jason's voice rose. 'This is my son you're talking about! Not about whether you stole the last biscuit out of the jar. Tammy, that is just a lame excuse.' He stood abruptly and paced around the room. 'Is that how you justify what you have done?' He would make sure Tammy knew just how angry he was.

'I've said I am sorry.' Tammy felt the tears pricking the backs of her eyes. She couldn't blame him for being angry. She had made such a mess of everything. 'I know nothing I can say will replace the time you two have lost because of my actions.'

'You're damn right there.' Jason tried keeping his voice even, but it was difficult as his anger boiled and bubbled away inside his veins.

'Jason, what do you want me to say?' Her voice was barely more than a whisper.

'The truth may be a good place to start!' Jason demanded. 'Why did you hide him from me, from my mum and dad?'

'Toby's mine. You're not having him.' Her voice filled with panic as she wrapped her arms around herself.

'He isn't a possession. He is a little boy.' Jason was breathing heavily. 'He's my child, and in your wisdom you chose to hide him and lie, telling me his mother was dead. How many other people have you spun that line to? Or is it only me?'

'Just you. Everyone I know, knows Toby is my child.' She sighed heavily. 'I . . . I . . . '

But Jason wouldn't let her finish. He needed to say what he had come to say. 'Did I ever hurt you? Have I ever done anything to make you scared of me?' Jason's heart went out to her. He was angry, but right now Tammy looked so fragile as she sat huddled in the corner of the sofa. She looked just like a deer trapped in the headlights. Getting angry wasn't accomplishing anything. He had more questions than answers, and the angrier he got the more withdrawn from him she became.

'There is no excuse for what I have done; my only hope is that the two of you will have a relationship.' Wrapping her arms around her knees, Tammy knew deep down in her soul that she had lost Jason, and she could lose Toby because of her own selfish attitude. 'Toby seemed to enjoy the time he spent time with you.'

Jason calmed a little. 'I like spending time with him too.' Maybe it was time he changed tactics. 'You have done a great job of raising him on your own.'

Tammy went on the defensive. 'I had no choice but to raise him on my own. There was no one else who would have been bothered.' As soon as the words left her mouth she regretted them. It had been her choice to raise Toby on her own. Jason wasn't to blame for the mess; she was.

'That was your choice, Tammy! You took him out of my hands. How could I have helped him if I didn't know?' Jason kept his voice even.

Tammy knew he was right but it wasn't going to change matters, especially when they weren't doing anything other than getting angry at each other.

Jason picked up a photo album, trying his best to calm the situation. He couldn't excuse what Tammy had done, but he wasn't going to let his family go either. He still loved her despite her egregious error of judgement. 'Why don't we look through the photo albums together? You can explain where they have been taken.'

'They have all got labels attached to them.'

She was organised, he thought. On opening one of the heavy albums, Jason saw she had indeed marked them all out and placed a small label on each with information about where it had been taken and the date.

'There are only so many albums because I used one picture per page, just so you would know where they had been taken. I even added a little description as well. Everything Toby has ever done is within these pages for you.'

'Would you have ever given them to me?' Jason studied her face but he couldn't read her.

'One day I would have done.' There, she had said it. She couldn't have hidden Toby forever — just long enough for Jason to leave again. 'I must admit that I wanted you to go back into the army without you finding out. I hadn't anticipated on wanting you or falling in love with you all over again.' The last thing Tammy was going to

301

admit was that she had always loved him. She had never stopped.

'Was I so awful to you, that you could just turn your back on everything we had?' Jason had no idea what had caused them to break up. He had loved her then, but felt he wasn't able to provide for her properly with an under gardener's wage. He had wanted to enlist and provide them with a better future together, but Tammy couldn't or didn't want to wait for him.

'Did you just say . . . ' Jason stopped abruptly as he tried to process the comment she had sneaked out. 'You, love me?'

'Yes,' she mumbled. Tammy took a deep breath as she realised she could no longer hide. Jason was right: Toby wasn't a cookie, and the lies she had told had hurt everyone she loved. It was time to tell the full truth. 'I fell pregnant just before you went into the army.' Letting out a huge sigh, she realised it was going to be hard for her to tell him her reasons. They sounded so ridiculous now. 'I knew how much you wanted to join up, to serve your country, and I felt that I was just standing in your way.' Tammy buried her face in her hands, her body shaking with tears.

'How could you have ever stood in my way?' Jason was confused. Was that really what she thought? 'We could have stayed together.' Didn't Tammy know just how much he had wanted that? 'I would have been home on leave and we could have been happy. They have couples' accommodation; we could have got one of those.' Well, it was true that not everyone was cut out to be a soldier's wife.

Tammy shook her head. 'No, Jason, I had to let you go. If you knew I was pregnant, would you have gone? Or would you have stayed here with us?'

Jason looked at her. Of course he would have stayed; what on earth had she been thinking? His duty would have been to his child and his girlfriend. 'I would have stayed and taken care of you.'

'You would have resented me after a while.' Tammy knew it was true, as he had been so adamant about joining the army. 'I didn't want to be the reason you gave up your dream.' She tried to stop her lip trembling. 'I told you he was Debbie's so you would carry on as before — following your dream and becoming an officer.'

Watching Tammy standing and wandering around the room, Jason realised that she believed she had to put some distance between them by creating a barrier. He sent shivers down her spine. 'I have always loved you,' she said. 'But it was the right decision at the time, or at least it felt like it was.'

Jason sat on the sofa, looking up at her. 'Tam, sit down.' Tammy slowly walked back to the sofa and did so. Jason placed his arm around her shoulders and brought her close to him. She sobbed softly into his chest. 'Tam, I thought you were unhappy.' So that was it — the reason for her actions was so that he could do what he had always wanted. 'It crossed my mind that you had found someone else to love. Who made you happier than you ever could be with me.'

Shaking her head, Tammy said, 'Oh no, Jason. Don't ever think that, please. Don't ever think I didn't love you.' Tears fell down her face. 'That I stopped loving you. Letting you go was the hardest decision I ever made. I needed you with me, with our child.' Tammy turned her face to his to judge his reaction, but he stared blankly back at her. 'I never meant to hurt you.' All she had done was hurt herself, and as far as she could see he was blameless in all of it. 'Then when Debbie died I was totally on my own.' She added silently, *You didn't want me; you needed to go away and live your life.* 'You had outgrown River Springs, Jason.' She couldn't look him in the eye and concentrated on her hands instead. 'You had outgrown me. I didn't want you to think I had trapped you into marriage or having a baby you didn't want,' she added, her voice barely audible.

'Tammy all you had to do was ask me to stay.' Jason's voice was tinged with sadness. He didn't bother waiting for a reply. Placing a finger under her chin, he tilted her head up towards him. He pressed his lips hard against her mouth, devouring its softness, setting her body aflame with his punishing and angry kiss. He enveloped her in his arms as he deepened the kiss, seeking entrance to her mouth with his tongue.

Tammy was surprised at her own passionate response to him as her stomach whirled around; her over-sensitive skin burned to his touch. She couldn't think straight. All that mattered was the way Jason was kissing her, and his touch as he twirled her hair around in his fingers.

Jason broke away and tilted her head to face him as he whispered, 'I love you, Tam. I never want to be without you.'

He paused for a moment. 'I need you; I need both of you in my life.' He realised just how stupid it had all been. He wasn't sure they could make things work, but he wasn't going to give up without a fight. Tammy was the other part of him. She had been ingrained in his head and heart for so long. 'You should never have thought I didn't want you.'

Jason realised that no matter what he had done, his life seemed empty, not having anyone to share things with except his parents. He knew that every girl he had dated he had compared to the girl sat before him.

A lump formed in Tammy's throat. After everything that had happened between them, all she could think of was how happy she was going to be. 'I love you too, Jason.' Suddenly her eyes filled with tears. 'I'm so sorry Jason, I'm so sorry.' Sobs racked Tammy's body as years of grief and guilt came pouring out of her.

Jason placed a finger to her mouth

'Ssh darling, it doesn't matter now.' As they sat together he wondered just how far he could go. Had she loved him as he had always loved her? No matter where he had gone in the world, Tammy had always been there. A small voice in his head would appear whenever he felt homesick, and he would find Tammy and go back to a time when they had been young and carefree. He loved the way she melted into his body as they clung to each other on the sofa.

Suddenly Tammy looked up at him. 'Why are you dressed as a fireman?'

'You are looking at the newest trainee for the River Springs Fire Service,' he said proudly.

'Toby will be impressed. His very own fireman!' Tammy grinned. She liked a man in uniform.

Jason gave her his cheekiest smile. 'Would you like me to turn around so you can stare at my ass a bit more?' He saw Tammy blush at his suggestion, then jumped up suddenly. 'Come on, let's get out of here.'

It had taken Jason a while to realise that in her own particular way Tammy had tried to do the right thing by him, but had only ended up hurting them both. He wanted to raise Toby as a family and maybe even make a few more Tobys. This time he intended to do the right thing.

'Where?' Tammy asked, her voice quivery.

Jason smiled when he saw the confused look on Tammy's face. 'Just out. Do you trust me?'

'I guess so, although I am not sure what you are up to,' she said, her voice still shaky.

Jason grabbed her jacket on the way out of the door. He had an idea but wasn't sure he could pull it off. He knew he was totally besotted with her. He had tried to stop himself falling in love with her but it had been totally futile to resist. It was time they both let go of the past, put all the hurt and accusations behind them, and moved on. If that was possible. Could Tammy do that? Could she let go of her guilt?

'Get in,' he urged as he opened the car door.

Tammy wasn't really paying attention to where they were going. They drove along the main road out of town and deep into the countryside. The concrete jungle was replaced by sprawling hills and livestock. The last of the sweet-smelling heather was turning a coarse brown colour. Every so often a clump of rich purple heather peeped its head up and still sat majestically amidst the carpet of brown. The leaves floated softly and silently to the ground in a rainbow of different hues.

Jason pulled into the a car park at the edge of a sprawling wood. Large fir and pine trees guarded the entrance like soldiers on guard duty. 'Come on.'

'But . . . ' Tammy instantly recognised where they were. Surprise View was just around the bend; they had gone there for one of their first dates. It had been a picnic at the height of summer, and they had watched as walkers and sheep passed them by. It was a stark contrast to the noise of the town; they had removed themselves to a more secluded spot, wanting privacy. They had sat on a rock jutting out from the hillside, with only abandoned millstones for company. They had kissed, and for the first time Jason had told Tammy he loved her. Tammy smiled at the memories. Her tears had dried, and with her breathing now back to normal, a strange sort of tranquillity had settled over her. Why now, after all this time, had he brought her back out here?

'Do you know why we've come here?' Jason prodded.

'For the fresh air?' came Tammy's light-hearted reply.

'Don't you remember?'

A blush spread over Tammy's cheeks as she nodded. She had been thinking the very thing that he was. How different it had been several years before. Tammy would give anything to have that back. For Jason to forgive her and just to be hers. Maybe bringing her here was his way of saying that he had forgiven her for everything; or was it just for Toby that he was doing it? After all, it was so much better if you could get on for the sake of the children. The mischievous look on his face warned her that he was probably up to his old tricks again.

'Come on.' Jason grabbed her hand. Feeling the warmth of her skin next to his sent shivers down his spine. They wandered in silence as slowly they made their way back to the same rock where it had all begun. 'Sit down, Tam.' The stone was ice-cold; there was not enough sun this time to warm the surface.

'Why are we here?' Tammy asked.

'Well, I have got something to say and I thought we both needed to get out of River Springs for a while.'

The confusion on Tammy's face was just what Jason wished to see. After the argument this morning he wasn't at all sure how it would all go, but he didn't care. Tammy was going to be his. They had lost so much time already, and he intended that they make it up and a whole lot more besides. What the hell, he thought, and reaching into his pocket he produced a small black velvet box. Ever so slowly he opened the lid to reveal a diamond ring.

'Marry me, Tam!' He had bought the ring when he had returned from the barracks. He had known then just how much Tammy meant to him, and he wasn't going to let her go. She was the only woman for him. He was just waiting for the right time, but it hadn't come, and then Tammy's revelation had ripped his dreams apart. The soldier in him told him not to give up, that there was a reason behind her madness and he just had to find out what it was. Even now it seemed like the most stupid thing on earth to have done, but that was Tammy all over — she didn't always think before she acted.

Tammy was numb. She couldn't believe that after everything she had done, Jason wanted to marry her. No words could express how she felt and with just a nod of her head, Tammy allowed Jason to place the ring on her finger, while they looked into each other's eyes and shared a soft and gentle kiss. They sat for several minutes in total silence, holding on to each other, both thinking just how far they had come.

Tammy had nearly lost everything by pushing Jason away because she thought it was the right thing to do. Now she had a second chance at happiness and she was determined to grab it with both hands.

'Come on, Tam, let's go to the station and tell everyone. I want to shout it from the rooftops that you're mine.'

'What about telling our parents first? I'm sure they going to be shocked,' Tammy replied.

'You're right,' Jason admitted. 'Then we will go to the station.'

Jason took her hand and pulled her up off the rock. As he held her tightly, they surveyed the view; it was so peaceful and quiet. The only thing that Jason could hear was the sound of their hearts beating. He smiled inwardly. He would give Tammy a shock and really shout it from the rooftops, or at least the fire station roof.

12

Six months later

Tammy woke up with a slight headache from all the wine that she and Jason's mum Blossom had drunk the night before. She dreaded to think about the mess they had created downstairs after their girly night, and glancing at the clock she saw that the time had slipped by. They had only two hours to get their hair done, get dressed, and arrive at the church on time.

Tammy looked around the room as she came to and saw her white wedding dress hanging on the door of the wardrobe. She went off in search of Toby but found the bed empty. Wandering downstairs, she heard the noise of the TV. *Well at least I know where he is.* Tammy headed into the front room and saw her son lying on a cushion on the floor, watching cartoons. 'Toby, it's time to get dressed now, darling.'

Toby turned around. 'But Mum, can't I finish watching this film? It's really good.' He was soon staring at the TV screen again.

'I'm sorry, darling, but we will be late if we don't get a move on. We have all slept in. So we are already running late.'

A knock at the front door sent her into a panic. The photographer had arrived to take some pictures of them all in the house as they prepared for her big day. Yet here they all were, running around with their PJs on. Not a bridesmaid or bride in sight. Tammy laughed at the poor photographer stood on the doorstep, dumbfounded as he saw a woman in her PJs standing in front of him.

The house was sent into a flurry of activity as everyone rushed around getting ready. They crashed into each other on the stairs and landing, grabbing a cup of tea and a piece of toast when they could — not that Tammy herself had much of an appetite. The doorbell rang constantly, hindering their progress as someone had to stop what they were doing and answer it, taking cards from well-wishers.

An elderly lady stood in the doorway wearing a peacock-blue two-piece, a hat covering her salt-and-pepper hair. Tammy hugged the old lady. 'Gran, you've turned up just in time. Could you please answer the door and the phone if it rings?'

'Of course, darling. You go make yourself pretty for that nice young man,' she said, shooing her grand-daughter upstairs.

A stream of well-wishers came just to drop off cards for the happy couple, many of whom were going to be at the wedding but were determined to be the first ones to glimpse the bride-to-be, in all her finery. Her gran made sure that they all wandered away and were left extremely disappointed; they, like everyone else, would have to wait for her to arrive at the church.

Blossom walked into Tammy's bedroom and let out a gasp. 'You look beautiful, darling.' Her son's future wife had quite taken her breath away. Tammy looked at herself in the full-length mirror. She was wearing a white taffeta dress and a crystal tiara; a traditional veil completed the look.

The hairdresser put most of her hair up, twisting it into tight curls and leaving just a few loose tendrils dangling onto her shoulders. The bride and bridesmaids carried posies of pink and white roses to finish off the picture.

'Tammy, there's just something missing,' Aunt Mary told her.

'I think I have everything. I've borrowed my bracelet, my dress is new, and I made sure to get a blue garter,' Tammy replied.

'You've forgotten something old.' Aunt Mary unfastened her teardrop pearl necklace. 'Here, wear this. It completes the tradition.'

Tammy recognised it instantly and tried to give it back. 'I can't. It was Debbie's,' she whispered.

'Please don't cry. You will smudge your makeup. Panda eyes are not attractive. Besides, I know she would have been happy for you to have it,' replied her aunt in a reassuring tone. Tammy allowed her to fasten the necklace around her neck. Mrs Mathews stood slightly back away from Tammy so that she could admire the sight before her. 'There, now you are ready.'

'Thank you, Aunt Mary.' Tammy fingered the pearls gently. 'It means so much to me.'

Tammy heard her father shouting up the stairs. 'The cars are here, darling.'

'Come on, Tammy, it's time to get you married,' Blossom said, urging her new daughter-in-law to get a move on. Tammy looked as Toby proceeded down the stairs in front of them, wearing a grey morning suit. Several of the neighbours stood lining both sides of the garden path, waiting for her to get into the car.

Tammy struggled to get into the white limousine, her foot-long train getting in the way. She stifled a giggle as she ungraciously sat down on the car seat, showing her garter to the handful of people that had stayed around to watch. Mr Morgan sat gingerly beside his daughter, being careful not to crush her dress. Toby and Tammy's mother got into the black Rolls Royce Phantom behind the wedding car with Jason's mother.

'You look so beautiful! I'm so proud of you, darling,' her dad told her.

'Thanks, Dad' Tammy replied as she gently wiped the tear from her father's face.

'It's going to be a great day all round.'

Tammy beamed. 'I'm sure it will, Dad. Thanks for everything.'

They arrived fashionably late to the church. Getting out of the limousine again was just as eventful as it was getting into it.

Tammy stood behind the old oak doors of the church and waited impatiently for the organist to start playing. When the first chords of Mendelssohn's 'Wedding March' began, they all took their positions in the order they would walk down the aisle. Toby went first, carrying the rings on a white satin pillow, and Jason's niece scattered rose petals along the aisle for the bride to walk on. Then Tammy and her father followed behind. She couldn't remember much of the ceremony; it all went by so quickly and she was still in a daze. The only thing she remembered was people coming up to her to congratulate the happy couple as they made their way to Chatsworth Hotel for the reception and wedding photos. Tammy had actually married Jason — and that, she couldn't believe.

Looking around the reception hall, Tammy spotted two wedding cakes: the chocolate one they had chosen for Toby in the shape of a fire engine, and the three-tired red velvet one she herself had fallen in love with. The chocolate roses climbing up the side of the cake had been a nice touch.

As the groom led his bride onto the dance floor, Bonnie Tyler's hit 'Total Eclipse of the Heart' started to play.

Jason placed his arms around her, bringing her in close. 'I love you Tam. You've made me so happy.'

'I love you too. Thank you; I couldn't have asked for a nicer wedding than this.' Tammy sobbed with tears of joy.

Jason leaned over and kissed his bride, knowing that at last he had received his own miracle: a family, one he hadn't been sure he could ever have. He had his entire future right there in his arms.

THE END

NIGHT MUSIC

Margaret Mounsdon

Marian and Georges, world-famous stars of classical music, are very much in love — though neither knows much about the other's past. One freezing night, while sheltering with Georges from a blizzard in an old barn, Marian's deepest secret comes back to haunt her in the most unexpected way, and she soon finds herself in danger from a stalker and a psychopath as she struggles to put together the missing pieces of her life. Will Georges still love her in the end — if they both make it through alive?

THE APOTHECARY'S DAUGHTER

June Davies

Keziah Sephton is kept busy caring for three generations of her family, as well as running the family apothecary shop. George Cunliffe has loved Keziah since they were youngsters, and when Benedict Clay arrives at the shop claiming to be blood kin, and is welcomed into the heart of the family, George is immediately suspicious of the soft-spoken Southern gentleman's motives ... After her grandmother's precious Book of Hours disappears, Keziah is tormented by treacherous doubts and swiftly enmeshed in a shocking spiral of deception, betrayal, ruthless ambition — and cold-blooded murder.

HOUSE OF DREAMS

Fenella J. Miller

In the small Cornish village of Tregorran, Demelza struggles to keep the family house intact and care for her young brothers and sister after the deaths of her parents. Knowing that she is losing the battle, she agrees to take in a paying guest: handsome Lucas Fairfield. But the growing attraction between the two seems doomed from the start. With Lucas obliged to return to his ancestral manor in Hampshire, and Demelza devoted to caring for her siblings and own familial home in Tregorran, can they ever find happiness together?

GRACE'S COTTAGE

Noelene Jenkinson

Jennifer is a small-town girl living with, and caring for, her invalid mother and wayward sister. Sam is an architect from the big city, brooding over a dark secret from his past. When Sam visits the café where Jennifer works, she is less than impressed with his brusque manner. However, as a series of events throws them together, their growing attraction is undeniable. Can the two of them overcome the considerable difficulties that stand in the way of their happiness together, or will they be forced to go their separate ways?

TAKE MY BREATH AWAY

Sally Quilford

During the 50th anniversary remake of *Cleopatra*, movie star Patty Carter's ex-husband Jason is found dead in his trailer with a knife in his chest. No one seems to be safe as the murderer strikes again and again. Whilst fighting off suspicions that she is the killer, Patty is torn between handsome insurance investigator Tony Marcus and equally handsome actor Matt Archer. But Patty is keeping back a secret about Jason, and Tony is determined to discover the truth, even if he is falling desperately in love with her . . .